bm.

'Christy,' he said softly.

He looked down at her and smiled and there was no one in Christy's world but Adam.

This couldn't be happening. She was no longer a lovesick student. Christy Blair was twenty-six, a professional pharmacist and a woman of sense. She had to get a grip on herself.

'Hello, Dr McCormack,' she said stiffly, holding her hand out in formal greeting. 'My brother asked me to meet you.'

Dear Reader

We continue with our quartet, LONG HOT SUMMER, in which Babs starts work in the rehabilitation unit, and complete the Lennox duet with LEGACY OF SHADOWS, where Christy has to face her past. Jenny Ashe takes us to Singapore, an area she knows well, in IN THE HEAT OF THE SUN, and from Caroline Anderson we have PICKING UP THE PIECES. Nick, in her previous book SECOND THOUGHTS, demanded his own story, and this is it. Just what you need in cold February to warm you. Enjoy!

The Editor

Marion Lennox has had a variety of careers — medical receptionist, computer programmer and teacher. Married, with two young children, she now lives in rural Victoria, Australia. Her wish for an occupation which would allow her to remain at home with her children, her dog and the budgie led her to attempt writing a novel.

Recent titles by the same author:

A LOVING LEGACY
THE LAST EDEN

LEGACY OF SHADOWS

BY

MARION LENNOX

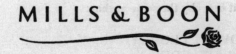

MILLS & BOON LIMITED
ETON HOUSE, 18–24 PARADISE ROAD
RICHMOND, SURREY, TW9 1SR

*First published in Great Britain 1993
by Mills & Boon Limited*

© Marion Lennox 1993

*Australian copyright 1993
Philippine copyright 1994
This edition 1994*

ISBN 0 263 78474 6

*Set in 10 on 10½ pt Linotron Times
03-9402-58368*

*Typeset in Great Britain by Centracet, Cambridge
Made and printed in Great Britain*

CHAPTER ONE

'RICHARD, there must be a million doctors in the world to choose from. You can't possibly want Adam McCormack!' Christy leaned against the cluttered pharmaceutical counter and gazed at her brother in horror. He had to be joking!

Dr Blair smiled, fleetingly easing the fatigue from his eyes. He looked at his sister with affection. With Christy's slim figure, freckles and wide blue eyes it was hard for him to accept she was a grown woman and a qualified pharmacist.

'The other ninety-nine thousand or so are all busy this week.'

'Don't try and be funny.' Christy dug her hands deep into the pockets of her white overall while her mind spun into blind panic. Richard had more urgent things to consider than his sister's reaction to his future partner. How could she make him understand? 'Richard, you can't do this,' she said finally. She shook her head, her face losing some of its colour at what Richard was suggesting. Adam McCormack! Adam. . .

Richard sighed and his smile slipped. 'Christy, I know you didn't hit it off with Adam McCormack the last time you met. But that was years ago, for heaven's sake. You were just a kid. He probably doesn't even remember you.'

'I was twenty-one, Richard.' Christy closed her eyes bleakly. 'I was not a kid. And it doesn't matter whether he remembers me. I remember him.'

Christy remembered Adam McCormack only too well. Richard had brought him home for a week's holiday five years ago. When Christy arrived home from university, both Richard and Christy's mother

5

had asked her to be nice to their visitor — Dr Adam McCormack. 'He's had a tough time,' they'd told her. Well, Christy had tried, and she still remembered the results with horror.

'He didn't even tell me. . .' She muttered, her pale cheeks turning crimson in remembrance.

'That he was married?' Richard shook his head in irritation. 'I imagine he thought I'd told you. And really, Christy, if I'd thought you were going to make a fool of yourself over the man I would have.' He shrugged. 'Anyway, Adam McCormack was too caught up in his own personal tragedy to be aware of you flaunting yourself in front of him. . .'

'I did not flaunt! You told me to be nice. . .'

'Flaunt,' Richard said decisively. He smiled again. 'In fact it probably did Adam good, and five years is a long time to remember a friend's sister's calf love.'

Christy's colour deepened. She cast a look up at her brother's amused face and looked down again. It had seemed amusing to Richard at the time. To all of them. No doubt it was amusing to Adam himself. What they didn't know — none of them — was just how deeply it had affected her.

'He's coming, Christy,' Richard said relentlessly. 'Look, love, I haven't a choice. Kate is not fit to practise. The baby's due any day and with the hospital, the surgery and the nursing home Corrook needs three doctors, not one. I'm run into the ground and Adam's offer is the answer to a prayer. He wrote and said he wanted a change and wouldn't mind trying country practice in Australia if I knew of an opening. I rang him last night to say he could start today if he could get here in time.'

'Today!'

'Well, he can't, of course,' Richard sighed. 'But he said he could be here by Sunday. Which brings me to my next request, Christy, dear. . .'

Christy knew that tone of voice. She walked into the

dispensary and locked the narcotics cupboard. It was Friday night, and it was starting to look like the beginning of a very long weekend.

'What do you want?' she demanded. She tucked her unruly blonde curls behind her ears and took off her white coat, hanging it behind the door to the dispensary. It was almost as if she was shrugging off the trappings of Christy Blair, pharmacist, so that Christy Blair, Richard's sister, could hold sway. As a pharmacist she had to be civil to Dr Blair, but Richard's sister was under no such obligation.

'Christy, Adam's flight gets into Melbourne at two on Sunday afternoon. Seeing you're not working. . .'

'No!' Christy placed her fist down on the counter with a thump, making the jars and boxes on the wooden counter jump. 'Richard, you can't ask that of me. If you want him then you meet him.'

'How can I, Christy?' Richard asked reasonably. 'I'm the only doctor in the place apart from Kate, and if Kate goes into labour. . .' He stopped and the worry lines stretched tighter. 'I wish to hell she'd go to Melbourne and stay with her parents.'

Christy shook her head. 'Kate says the baby's not due for two weeks. She says first babies never come on time so she'll go when she's due and not before.'

'You know as well as I that she's saying what she wants to believe.' Richard dug his hands into his pockets in a gesture that matched his sister's. Physically the two were as different in appearance as siblings could be, but they were alike none the less. Richard met Christy's eyes and knew she would do what he asked. She was darn near as fond of Kate as he was.

'But to meet Adam McCormack. . .' Christy's voice was practically a wail. 'Richard, it's not fair. I don't ever want to see the man again. You can't ask me. . .'

'Are you two arguing again?' The woman's voice caused Christy to turn. Unnoticed, her sister-in-law had entered and stood watching her husband and

Christy. 'What's he trying to bludgeon you into, Christy?'

Christy took a deep breath and let it out in a sigh of frustration. Kate looked more weary than Richard. The baby hung heavily on her over-thin body and Kate put her hands to the small of her back as she talked in an unconscious gesture of discomfort.

Richard said the baby could come any day. If Christy refused to meet Adam from the plane then Richard would be away from Corrook for at least eight hours. Eight hours was a long time where babies were concerned and there was no way Christy intended delivering Kate's baby. Pharmacy training had its limits.

'Richard wants me to meet Dr McCormack on Sunday,' Christy said shortly.

'And you can't?' Kate's smile of greeting faltered. She looked over at her husband and her smile slipped further. 'Richard, you'll have to go, then. I. . . I can manage here. . .'

Christy held up her hands in defeat. 'You know very well that the most likely medical need in the valley on Sunday will be your baby arriving, Kate, and you can hardly deliver it yourself.'

'Women have done it before,' Kate smiled. 'Not that I'd like to try.'

Christy sighed again. 'OK, Richard. You win. I'll meet your precious new partner from the plane. But I tell you, Richard Blair, if he's the man I remember, you'll be looking for a new pharmacist for Corrook any day now. Corrook's a small town and I don't think it's big enough for both of us.'

Richard raised his eyebrows. 'You don't think you're being just a touch melodramatic?'

Christy directed a final glare at her brother. 'Take Kate home before she drops,' she ordered, ignoring his last remark. 'She looks as if she should be in bed.'

'I'm fine,' Kate protested. 'I wish you'd stop fussing.'

'It keeps my mind occupied,' Christy said savagely. 'It keeps me from thinking how much I'd like to murder my big brother.'

CHAPTER TWO

ADAM MCCORMACK. . . The name went through and through Christy's mind as she drove the last few miles to the airport on Sunday afternoon. Her little red sports car devoured the miles with ease and she lifted her foot fractionally from the accelerator. The last thing she wanted was to arrive early.

Adam McCormack. . . The flush had hardly died from her cheeks since she had heard he was coming. One of the advantages of migrating from England to join her brother in Australia had been that she would never have to run the risk of meeting the man again. And yet here she was, thousands of miles from home and about to be confronted with the pain she had known for five long years.

Would Adam have forgotten? Probably, she thought bitterly. After all, to him she had been a holiday distraction — to be enjoyed and then put aside gently as he went back to the things in his life that mattered. To Christy, though. . . To Christy Adam had been a curtain lifting on her cloistered life. She had never met anyone like him before and she had measured every male against him since.

No one had measured up. She had long ago lost her sense of proportion where Adam McCormack was concerned. Christy bit her lip as the outer suburbs of Melbourne slid by. Was he just some figment of her youthful fantasies? Maybe when she met him now she would see him as she should have seen him five years ago — a friend of her brother and an ordinary male. 'Just a man,' she said harshly to herself. 'I've had boyfriends since Adam McCormack. Nice ones too. Dr

10

Adam McCormack is nothing special. He can't hurt me. . .'

She didn't believe it. The roar of an aircraft as she approached the airport made her look up and a huge British Airways jet thundered over the highway ahead of her, heading to land at Tullamarine Airport. She glanced at her watch. It was just on two. That was Adam's plane.

'Let it crash,' she said savagely. 'Let a hole appear in the side and just one passenger be sucked to his doom. Just one passenger. . .'

You're being stupid, she told herself silently. Adam McCormack is someone you're going to have to face before you get on with the rest of your life. And if you have to do it, you might as well do it straight away.

Her foot came down on to the accelerator once again and the little car sped up to join the stream of traffic headed for the airport.

He didn't recognise her at first.

Christy stood in the crowd of people clustered around the door to the customs hall, waiting for Adam to emerge. Around her were people calling and waving, embracing arrivals with tearful hugs and kisses. Christy was jostled back and forth with the crowd, but her eyes never left the door to the customs hall. She saw Adam the moment he walked through the swinging door. She saw him and her hope that her memory had deceived her — that she could look at him and see nothing but a friend of Richard's and a future doctor for Corrook — faded to oblivion.

He was the same Adam. He was shorter than Richard — slightly under six feet and broadly built, with a frame that was suggestive of muscled strength. He was wearing tweeds, out of place here in the heat of an Australian summer, though they must have been sensible when he boarded the plane and they didn't look strange. Nothing on Adam McCormack would look strange, Christy decided. If he walked into a ballroom in flippers and snorkel he was the sort of male who would have everyone else in the ballroom wondering why they hadn't worn swimwear as well. He was a leader and it showed—in the cool green eyes sweeping impatiently over the crowd and the lean, long fingers pushing back his sandy-coloured hair in a gesture of time being wasted. A man in a hurry. . .

Why was he here? Christy wondered about his reasons for the hundredth time. Why had he suddenly decided to abandon England? He'd been practising as an obstetrician, she'd heard, with a successful practice in central London. General practice in Corrook was going to be vastly different.

At least his obstetric skills would ease Richard's worry about Kate, Christy knew, and the thought of her sister-in-law made her stir. Reluctantly she pushed her way through the crowd until she was within reach of Adam.

'Dr McCormack?' she said quietly. Then, as he didn't hear above the crowd and didn't turn towards her, she placed a hand tenatively on his tweed-covered arm, 'Adam?'

He turned then. Swinging around, he stared down at the girl who had touched him. His eyes narrowed. 'I don't. . .' He began and then his eyes widened again. The dark eyes creased into a smile. 'Christy,' he said softly.

It was the same heart-stopping smile. It did to Christy what it had done five years before. It made the world around her freeze. They might have been in a world apart. He looked down at her and smiled and there was no one in the world but Adam.

Her heart had stilled but her mind reacted in panic. This couldn't be happening. It might be the same Adam but it had to be a different Christy. She was no longer a lovesick student. Christy Blair was twenty-six, a

professional pharmacist and a woman of sense. She
had to get a grip on herself.

'Hello, Dr McCormack,' she said stiffly, holding her
hand out in formal greeting. 'My brother asked me to
meet you.'

Adam's smile faltered a little at her stilted, cool
words. The green eyes lost their momentary warmth
and he seemed to withdraw slightly. 'That was kind of
him,' he told Christy, and his sudden coolness matched
Christy's.

'Richard's wife, Kate, is the only other doctor in
Corrook and is due to have a baby at any moment,'
Christy went on, desperate for him to understand that
she was not meeting him by choice. 'Richard could
hardly be away for the whole day. My car's in the car
park. Shall we go?'

'I see.' Adam bent and picked up his suitcases which
he'd put down to shake her hand. Christy started
walking as soon as he picked them up and he had to
move fast to keep up with her. 'You live at Corrook as
well?' he asked as they moved swiftly towards the
entrance.

'I run the local pharmacy,' Christy said stiffly.

The smile returned, just a little. 'I knew you'd
completed pharmacy and come to Australia. I didn't
know your career ambition was a country-town
chemist.'

Christy bit her lip. The man made her feel so
gauche — as if she were twenty-one again. Still, the fact
that he had known of her finishing pharmacy and
migration gave her a faint tinge of warmth. Maybe
Richard had told him without being asked, or maybe —
just maybe — Adam had cared enough to enquire.

It didn't matter. It mustn't be allowed to matter.
Adam McCormack could mean nothing to her. She
gave a brisk nod and walked out of the main airport
doors towards the car park beyond.

The north wind hit them with a scorching blast the

moment they emerged from the air-conditioned terminal. Adam visibly recoiled. He stopped and put down his luggage, looking ruefully across at Christy's simple cotton dress.

'I knew it would be hot but I hadn't expected this.' Christy had stopped before crossing the road from the terminal to the car park. Adam removed his jacket, and then picked up his suitcases again. 'Whew!'

'You've obviously done your homework on what to expect,' she said scornfully.

Adam looked curiously across at her. Around them people were streaming in and out of the airport doors, detouring around Adam and his suitcases, but he ignored them. Once more he placed his luggage on the hot pavement and continued looking straight at Christy.

'I'm not imagining this, am I?' he said quietly.

'Imagining what?' She tapped her foot impatiently and looked at her watch.

'The hostility I'm feeling,' he continued. 'It's hardly a welcome I'm getting.'

'Were you expecting a welcome?'

'Your brother tells me Corrook is desperate for another doctor. Is that true?'

'It's true,' Christy said grudgingly. 'But I can't see what on earth would entice a successful city obstetrician to a place like Corrook.' She looked over at the heat haze rising off the tarmac of the car park. 'Now, if you're right to go. . .'

'Let's have this out first.' The man was immovable. He stood there, his deep green eyes assessing her as though he and she were alone and they had all the time in the world. 'What's eating you, Christy?'

'Nothing.' She hesitated. 'I. . . I only heard on Friday you were coming.'

'And you didn't want me to come?'

'No. Yes. . .' Christy took a deep breath. 'I was

surprised. I thought. . . I thought you and your wife
were settled in London.'

Adam's face stilled. There was a long silence.
Around them travellers detoured around the couple
with various levels of impatience.

'Sarah's dead,' Adam said at last. 'Did you think I'd
walked out on her?' The silence continued. 'Are you
judging me, Christy? Half the world does, it seems.
Have I come to Australia to have that judgement
follow me?' Then, wearily, Adam picked up his luggage
yet again. He strode on to the road and this time it was
Christy who was left to follow.

Sarah. . .dead. Christy had only met Sarah once but
the memory had burned into her soul. Sarah was a
laughing, vibrant woman who had burst into the Blairs'
home all those years ago, reclaiming her husband with
practised ease.

'I do hope I'm not intruding,' she had laughed,
tucking her arm possessively into her husband's and
watching Christy out of the side of her beautiful eyes.
'Adam thought I'd be in Italy until the end of the
month, but who could leave a man for so long without
missing him like crazy? They told me at the hospital
he'd be here. Could you put me up for the night or
should Adam and I take ourselves off to a hotel?'
She'd snuggled closer to Adam. 'On second thoughts
maybe we should go to a hotel, shouldn't we, darling?
We haven't seen each other for weeks.' She'd smiled
blissfully up to her stunned audience.

As Christy's lovely dress burst around her, Adam
had turned to Mrs Blair and apologised gravely. He
had avoided looking at Christy. Christy's pain had been
on view for all to see. It was raw and very real.

'Maybe that would be best,' he'd agreed. 'I'm sorry.
I thought when I came here that Sarah would be
occupied for my entire leave.'

And he and Sarah had gone.

And now Sarah was dead. And Adam was here. Doing what? Grieving for Sarah?

It couldn't matter to Christy. Adam McCormack could mean nothing to her. All she could allow herself to feel was formal sympathy.

'I. . . I'm sorry,' she said stiffly, moving swiftly to walk beside him. She had to struggle. His strides were twice the length of hers. 'How. . .how did she die? Car accident?'

'I'd rather not talk about it.' Adam paused at the intersection of two lanes of parked cars. 'Where's your car, Miss Blair?'

'At the end of this lane.' Christy's voice was subdued. 'And please. . .call me Christy.'

'Does having a dead wife mean I rate a slightly less bitter reception?' Adam's question was disinterested, as if Christy's cold welcome had washed over him and was of no importance. For a moment Christy felt a stab of bitter regret that she hadn't welcomed him warmly as a long-standing friend.

'This is my car,' she said dully, as they reached the end of the row.

Adam stopped short, staring at the sleek little sports car in surprise. Then he raised his eyebrows. 'I suppose I should have expected it,' he said, almost to himself. 'Surely this isn't a sensible car for the wilds of Corrook?'

'We have sealed roads,' Christy snapped. 'You're not going to a last outpost of civilisation.'

'I thought Corrook was two hundred miles from the city.'

'That's not far in Australian terms.' Christy opened her luggage compartment and looked doubtfully at Adam's two large suitcases. 'One of those is going to have to go on the rear seat.'

'I suppose I should be grateful you do have a rear seat.' Adam peered over the side. 'Good grief. Rear seating for midgets?'

'You're welcome to call a taxi or hire a car if you like.'

Adam looked thoughtfully at the slim girl before him, her blue eyes flashing anger. 'You'd rather I did, wouldn't you?' he said calmly.

'Yes,' Christy said bluntly. She was close to tears, the emotions of five years ago surging through her as if the raw hurt had been inflicted yesterday. 'Look, Dr McCormack, can we get this journey over as fast as possible? I didn't ask for the job of collecting you. My brother needs you and he asked me to collect you. Once we get to Corrook, though, you're on your own and apart from deciphering your prescriptions I intend to have as little as possible to do with you.'

Adam's eyebrows raised. His wide mouth curved into a slow and mocking smile. 'That sounds like a challenge, Miss Blair. . . Christy.'

'Well, it's not,' Christy said savagely. She swung herself too hard into the driver's seat and sat down with a thump. 'It's a promise.' She gunned the engine into life. 'Now let's go.'

It was a long drive from Melbourne back to Corrook. Christy had done the trip many times in the couple of years she had lived in Corrook, but it had never taken so long as this afternoon. If only somehow she could ease the tension between her and this man beside her.

She grimaced inwardly as she drove. She hadn't meant to get off to such a bad start; in fact it would be a disaster if she did. For all she wanted nothing to do with Adam, Corrook was too small for that to happen. Christy's work was providing the pharmaceutical needs of the Corrook doctors. If she wasn't on speaking terms with one of those doctors it would be impossible. She had to try to establish at least formal civility.

'Adam?'

'Mmm?' Adam sounded close to sleep.

'Look, I'm sorry,' she said slowly, casting a glance

over at him. He was lying back with his eyes closed, his face turned to the sun as if he was absorbing its warmth. 'I didn't mean to be rude.'

'So why were you?' Adam said without opening his eyes. 'Has big brother forced you to meet me and made you miss a desirable social engagement?'

Christy laughed without humour. What would this man say if she told him the true reason—that she'd fallen hopelessly in love with him five years before and she knew he still had the capacity to hurt her as no other man could?

'Let's just say I got out of bed on the wrong side,' she said softly. 'I'm not always so ill-humoured.'

'It's just as well. I imagine you wouldn't have much of a pharmacy if you treated your customers the way you treated me. Or have you a monopoly?'

'I'm the only chemist for forty miles,' Christy agreed. She managed a faint smile. 'So you see, I can be as grumpy as I want.'

'Lucky you.' Still Adam didn't open his eyes.

'I'm trying to be nice.'

'So I hear.' Adam folded his arms across his chest. 'Why bother now?'

Christy flushed. 'Look, I said I'm sorry.' She took a deep breath, fighting for control. She was so aware of him—of the size of him filling her tiny car. His shirt-sleeve was brushing the bare skin of her arm every time she changed gear and it was all she could do not to shudder. 'I was. . . I was taking a bad mood out on you and I had no right. Having said I'm sorry, can we . . .can we start again, please?'

Christy stared straight ahead at the road. The silence stretched endlessly in front of them, like the heat-hazed bitumen. Finally Christy glanced sideways at the silent man and found his eyes watching her, his dark lashes shading his deep-set eyes from the sun. She turned back swiftly to pay attention to the road, but not fast enough to miss the trace of laughter in his look.

'Apology accepted, then,' he said and Christy could hear laughter reflected in his voice. 'I'm not one to bear a grudge.' He settled back against the soft leather upholstery of her little car and folded his arms across his chest. It was as if he was enjoying her discomfiture. 'I'm getting sunburned, you know. My lily-white complexion's not used to this heat.'

His complexion didn't look lily-white. For all he had come straight from an English winter, he looked more tanned than Christy.

'There's sun-cream in the glove compartment,' Christy told him. 'Or if you like I can put the hood up.'

'Not on your life.' He reached forward and took the cream from its niche, rubbing it liberally on to his face. 'The thought of skin cancer doesn't worry you?'

'I'm wearing cream already,' Christy told him. 'Thank you for your concern.'

'You're welcome.' He sounded as though he was still laughing. 'You've been here for two years?'

'Yes.' Christy was finding it hard to speak normally. Adam's presence was almost overwhelming. She was forcing her voice to normality—at least, she hoped she was.

'As long as Richard?'

'Nearly.'

'Why did you come?'

Because of you, Christy felt like saying. Because after you I couldn't settle. I kept hoping one day. . . one day I'd meet you and Sarah would have magically ceased to exist and we'd fall into each other's arms. . . So finally I packed my bags and came three thousand miles only to have you appear and hardly remember me.

'I came because Richard was here, of course,' she said tightly. 'Corrook needed a pharmacist and it seemed like a golden opportunity.'

'A golden opportunity to escape England?'

'Of course not,' Christy snapped. She grimaced, striving for the calm she'd resolved on. The road came to T-junction. She slowed to a halt and then swung left. When she had the car straight she had herself under control as well. 'How about you?' she asked lightly. 'What's a respected London obstetrician doing coming to Corrook?'

'Richard needed me,' Adam said lightly.

'Oh, come on. . .'

'That was your reason,' he told her. 'And I'm sure it's as true for me as it was for you.'

'But. . .' Christy shook her head. 'It's not the same,' she said at last. 'For me Corrook was an opportunity. For you to go back into general practice. . .'

'I enjoy general practice.' Adam was staring straight ahead, but Christy had the impression he was seeing something that didn't lie in front of the car. 'I missed it. When Sarah died. . .'

'When did she die?' The question was out almost before Christy knew she was going to ask it, and she regretted it before she said the last word. To her surprise, though, Adam didn't withdraw.

'Six months ago,' he said slowly. 'Since then I've been. . . Well, I've been unsettled.' He shrugged and the slow, heart-stopping smile flickered over his face. 'So here I am.'

'For how long?'

Adam looked thoughtfully at the slight, fair girl beside him. 'Is that the problem?' he asked, raising his eyebrows in mock-enquiry. 'Do you see me as transient?'

Christy shook her head. 'I'm sure it has nothing to do with me what you are,' she said stiffly. 'But. . .but it's hard to practise properly in Corrook if you don't know the people and it can take a long time to get to know them.'

'So you think I shouldn't come unless I'm prepared to stay?'

'I didn't say that.'

'You didn't have to.' Once again the self-mocking, slow smile. Christy had her eyes on the road but she could sense the smile rather than see it. It caught at her and nearly pulled her in two. It was as much as she could do not to weep. 'Your criticism is noted,' he said gravely. 'I wouldn't have come to work with Richard if Richard hadn't said he was desperate. I wanted a locum position for a few months and asked Richard if he'd heard of anything. The next thing I knew he was pleading with me to come to Corrook. I didn't get the impression I was depriving any permanent doctor of a place.'

Christy shook her head reluctantly. 'He is desperate,' she admitted. 'With Kate having the baby. . .'

'Kate's a doctor, too you said?'

'Kate was sole doctor here before Richard came,' Christy explained. 'Since Richard arrived, though, they've built up the practice to the point where one doctor can't cope. Richard's opened the hospital and they've built the Souter nursing wing and day centre. Now instead of the district's elderly folk retiring to the city they're staying put, and the medical demands of the community have increased accordingly.'

He nodded. 'So I'm not likely to be needing my obstetrics.'

Christy shrugged. 'There always seem to be babies arriving,' she said. 'The hospital hasn't birth-unit status. Expectant mums are supposed to go to the city. We find lots of them are like, Kate, though. They won't go until the last minute and it means there's the odd bundle dropped at Corrook Hospital.'

'Charmingly put.' Adam smiled and the mockery faded momentarily from his eyes. 'I like catching bundles. What do we need to get birth-unit status?'

'An obstetrician,' Christy told him. 'If you decided
to be permanent. . .'

'Which you doubt.'

'If you prove to be permanent, then I guess Richard
will pull strings and get the hospital accredited for
births,' Christy said evenly, ignoring his interjection.
'That's a way down the track, though.'

'That's right.' Adam's voice was as even as her own.
He glanced across at her. 'Am I right in thinking you'll
be only too pleased for me not to be permanent?'

Christy took a deep breath. 'I. . . I'm sure I couldn't
care either way,' she said harshly. 'Corrook needs
another doctor and it might as well be you.'

'How very kind.' He raised his eyebrows and the
mocking smile returned. 'Is it a male thing, then,
Christy? Would any male doctor be getting this
reception?'

'Any male doctor as arrogant as you,' she snapped.
She caught her breath with irritation. 'Look, let's leave
the personal inquisition, shall we? I don't have to like
you and I don't expect you to like me. We don't have
to take the relationship any further.'

Adam nodded. He closed his eyes again and leaned
back.

'There's only one thing,' he said slowly as he settled
back.

'Which is?' Christy was flushed and angry. How
could she maintain any sort of dignity around this man?

He smiled. 'You still sound just as if you're throwing
out a challenge.'

CHAPTER THREE

CHRISTY opened her pharmacy on Monday morning with a feeling of foreboding. This week was likely to be difficult.

This month was likely to be difficult, she told herself dully. This year. . . How long would the man stay?'

She had dropped him off at Richard and Kate's house the previous day and left, ignoring Kate's pleas to say on to dinner. She didn't want to spend one moment longer with Adam McCormack than was absolutely necessary.

'What's wrong, Christy?' Kate asked as she waved her goodbye. 'Don't you like Adam? Richard seemed so pleased he was coming. I thought. . .' She stopped and frowned, fatigue washing over her face. 'I do so hope it turns out OK.'

'It well might,' Christy told her, swallowing her emotions in the need to take the look of worry from Kate's face. She gave her sister-in-law a swift hug. 'I'm just having an "off" day. PMT or something.'

'Richard tells me you've been suffering PMT since Friday.' Kate managed an unconvinced smile. 'You don't think you should see a doctor about it?'

'I would if I knew a good one,' Christy grinned. She swung into her little sports car and gunned the engine into life, relieved to be going home and leaving Kate with the responsibility of Adam. 'Let me know if you hear of someone good.'

'Adam's an obstetrician. I bet he knows all about women's problems.'

'I'll bet,' Christy muttered. Forcing a smile, she waved and took herself off.

She went home to her little cottage — the cottage

Kate had owned when she first came to Corrook—
poured herself a cool drink and then sat on the veranda
for a long time.

It was quiet in the early evening. The wattle birds
were squabbling somewhere up in the high eucalypts
around the house and an unseasonable frog was complaining about the heat under the house. Apart from
that there was silence. Normally Christy loved these
hot, still evenings, blessing for the thousandth time her
decision to come to Australia. Not now. Not with
Adam McCormack almost within stone's throw.

She had been dreadful, she knew. Her behaviour to
him had been inexcusable. Normally Christy was
bright, extrovert and bouncy. She made friends easily
and there was no one in the valley she didn't call her
friend. Even Alf, the grumpy old chemist whose pharmacy she had taken over, had taken to dropping in to
watch, criticise and enjoy this fresh-faced English girl
dispensing medicine and good humour in equal
measure.

So where had that good humour disappeared to
now? It had no place near Adam McCormack.

'It's not his fault I was a fool,' she told herself sadly.
'He couldn't know how much he hurt me.'

But he should have, a little voice inside her argued.
We spent nearly a week together. He made me
laugh. . . The night before Sarah came he kissed
me. . .

It was just a kiss. She realised that now. To Adam it
had been just a kiss, taken because his wife was not on
hand to be kissed instead. He couldn't know how much
she had wanted that kiss. 'Adam's probably kissed
hundreds of women before and since,' Christy said
aloud, bitterly. 'It's me who's the fool for not being
able to get on with my life. He didn't make any
promises. He only kissed me. . .'

She had put her drink down and went inside to
wander aimlessly around the house until it was time for

bed. Bed had been a waste of time, though. Sleep was not for Christy Blair.

And now it was Monday, and her working life with Adam was about to begin. Christy's eyes were shadowed and she'd applied make-up for the first time all summer. In the heat, make-up somehow seemed wrong, and she usually didn't bother.

Ruth, her shop assistant, eyed her curiously as she opened the doors of the pharmacy and hooked them back.

'Are you OK, Miss Blair?'

'I'm fine, thanks,' Christy said briefly. 'Can you repack the cosmetic counter while it's quiet?'

'Sure,' Ruth said cheerfully. 'I gather you've met the new doctor, though, miss?'

'Yes.' Christy walked straight through to the dispensary at the back, hoping to prevent further questions, but Ruth, eighteen and burning with curiosity, was not so easily silenced. She knelt on the floor, cleared off the row of moisturisers from the bottom shelf, raised her voice and kept on.

'My dad saw him last night,' Ruth informed her. 'He's staying at the pub.'

'The pub?' Christy frowned. The Corrook pub was not a particularly welcoming place to stay. In fact it only offered accommodation because the licensing laws required it. Occasionally it put up a drunk who was too far gone to drive home but for the most part its beds stayed empty. 'I thought he was going to stay with Dr Blair.'

'I thought so, too,' Ruth said happily. 'But he told Mrs Mayne at the pub that he didn't feel it appropriate to stay with Kate's baby so close.' She pursed her lips over a bottle of moisturiser with a shop-soiled label and put it aside. 'Mrs Mayne says it's very gentlemanly of him. My dad had a drink with him last night and says he's just the ticket. Whatever that means,' she added dubiously. 'Do you like him, Miss Blair?'

'I hardly know him.'

'Yeah, but Dad says you drove him from the airport and you should be able to tell from that.' She paused. 'Miss Blair, if I shift the arthritis aids down here, I could put the moisturiser up a bit. If people need the aids, then they'll look for them. We make more money on the moisturiser, and the good moisturiser's an impulse buy. Shouldn't it be up?'

'The people looking for the arthritis aids are those less likely to be able to stoop and search,' Christy said firmly. 'The aids stay up.' She was checking the narcotic cupboard, something she did routinely every morning, and again after completing work. She picked up the re-order chart and started writing. Monday morning was her quiet time.

Ruth sighed. 'OK,' she told a pile of thermal knee-wraps. 'You can stay up in reach.' Then, not deflected, she got right back on track. 'Tell me about Dr McCormack, though.'

'If your dad's met him then he'll be able to answer questions as well as I can,' Kate said repressively.

'Yeah.' Ruth put the last of the wraps up again and stood. 'He can tell me that he seems a "decent sort of bloke". I want to know the important stuff.'

'Like?'

'Like is he married?' Ruth said in exasperation. 'And how old is he?'

'Too old for you,' Christy grinned. 'Honestly, Ruth. . .'

'But how old?' Ruth flicked back her pert brown bob and put her nose in the air. 'I've always fancied older men.'

'He must be close on thirty-five,' Christy told her.

'Oh.' Ruth was momentarily silenced. 'I don't know about *that* old.' She sighed. 'If he's as old as that he'll be married or divorced and have tribes of kids back in England or something.'

Children. . . Christy hadn't thought of that. She

wrote the next item on her list. . . Murelax. . . She stared down and then bit her lip. According to her list Murelax had been ordered three times. She flung the list down in disgust. Damn the man.

'I'm going to wash the front windows,' she told Ruth.

'But that's my job,' Ruth said in surprise. 'Honestly, Miss Blair, I was about to do it.'

'You vacuum,' Christy said firmly. 'I need some exercise.'

The phone cut across her words. Christy picked it up almost thankfully and then came close to dropping it as she realised who was on the other end of the line.

'Christy?'

Christy caught her breath. So it was starting. 'Blair Pharmacy,' she managed.

'Sorry,' Adam apologised drily. 'Good morning, Blair Pharmacy. Could Blair Pharmacy tell me what quantity Canesten comes in?'

'I. . . I beg your pardon?'

There was an exasperated sigh from the end of the phone. 'Like it or not, I need your help here, Miss Blair. I've been thrown in at the deep end. Richard's out on a house call and I'm the only one at the surgery. Richard's not answering his mobile phone. He must be out of range or suturing or something. I've Mr Hunstable in the surgery with tinea on his feet and I'm darned if I can find any list of prescription quantities. I've pulled the surgery apart looking.'

Christy smiled despite herself, feeling the first faint twinge of sympathy for Adam. It must be one heck of a shock to go from a city specialist practice to prescribing fungal cream for Mr Hunstable's feet.

'It comes in a twenty-gram tube,' she told him. 'You need a Mims.'

'Pardon?'

'A Mims.' Christy looked round at the shelf behind her and caught sight of the big blue volume. 'It's the Australian list of approved drugs. You also need a

Pharmaceutical Benefits List to check for the free list.
I can't understand why Richard didn't give them to
you.' For Adam to practise without the book would be
impossible.

'He doesn't know I'm working.'

Christy's frown deepened. She was aware of Ruth,
staring wide-eyed and openly interested. 'Why not?'

'He was showing me round the surgery when he had
an urgent call-out. I elected to stay behind and unpack
my gear. After an hour with no Richard I discovered
there were ten people in the waiting-room. I've managed four.'

'I'll send Ruth around with the book now.'

'Who's Ruth?' He sounded totally out of his depth
and Christy couldn't suppress a smile. It was just as
well the telephone didn't have a visual connection. For
a moment, for just a moment, Adam McCormack was
suffering. The feeling was good.

'Ruth's my assistant,' she told him. 'I wouldn't worry
about Ruth, though.' Her sense of humour surfaced
through the tension. She smiled across at her horrified
assistant. 'You're much too old.' She hung up.

'Ruth,' she said, 'your wish is about to come true.'
She retrieved the blue book and tossed it over. 'Off
you go and deliver this in person to Corrook's most
eligible bachelor.'

The phone shrilled again behind her. As Ruth
walked out of the shop, Christy picked up the receiver
yet again.

'I hadn't finished,' Adam said.

'Sorry, sir.' Christy bit back the urge to salute. 'How
may I help you further, Dr McCormack?' she said
meekly.

Adam sighed. 'Will the Mims be long?'

'Allowing for window-shopping on the way, Ruth
should be at the surgery in less than three minutes.'

'Are you doing anything for lunch?'

Christy almost dropped the receiver. When she

recovered she stared down as though the thing had
bitten her. He had to be joking.

'I'm having a sandwich here,' she said severely. 'If
there's no qualified pharmacist on the premises the
pharmacy has to shut. I run a business, Dr
McCormack.' Her voice was icy.

'Damn.'

Christy frowned. His expletive was of a man annoyed
rather than a man disappointed.

'Is there anything further you need? I have work to
do,' she said severely.

'Yes.' There was a moment's hesitation. 'Christy,
Richard tells me you might consider a boarder.'

'A boarder?'

'A paying house guest,' Adam said patiently. 'I
meant to ask you over lunch.' He sighed. 'Christy, I
can't stay with Richard and Kate. You must be able to
see that. I'd assumed I'd be able to stay at a hotel until
I could rent a place. But the hotel. . .' He sighed again.
'I had less than four hours' sleep last night and then
had to cope with Mrs Mayne's ingrown toenails over
steak and chips for breakfast. There are limits to what
a man can take.'

'I'm sure there are.' Christy's thoughts were racing.
She turned over in her mind the possible sources of
accommodation for Adam and reached the same con-
clusion as he had.

'There's nothing,' he told her. 'I rang the real-estate
agent first thing. There's a cottage in town becoming
vacant in a few weeks and a farm house fifteen miles
out. The road's terrible, and if I'm to be any help to
Richard I have to be accessible.'

'There's no room at the hospital?' Christy's mind
was twisting like a cornered animal. What Adam
McCormack was asking was appalling.

'There's a staffroom at the back but Mrs Brady's
staying there while Mr Brady recovers from a fractured

hip. Richard seems to think she'll need the room for a month. She's too nervous to stay home by herself.'

'So you want to move in with me?'

'Richard says you have heaps of room.'

'Damn Richard,' Christy exploded. 'Richard Blair has a lot to answer for. I suppose he's already dropped your belongings off on my front veranda.'

'They're still at the pub.' Adam's words were meek but there was still the trace of mocking laughter behind them. 'Christy, I'm a very quiet house guest.'

'I don't want a house guest.'

'Think of me as security. I keep thieves and rapists at bay.'

'I'd prefer thieves and rapists!'

'How can you say that?' Adam demanded, wounded. 'I make better coffee than any thief or rapist you've ever met.'

Despite her shock, Christy gave a choke of laughter, and as she did she was lost.

'I drink tea,' she said desperately but it sounded trite even to her ears and she heard the smile of satisfaction in Adam's voice as he responded.

'Earl Grey or Irish Breakfast? I make either, at seven every morning. With toast and real English marmalade, delivered hot to your bedside table.'

Christy drew in her breath. She had lost the battle and she knew it.

'Every morning?' she said dubiously.

'Cross my heart and hope to break a leg.'

'I wish you would,' she said desperately. 'Dr McCormack. . .'

'My Mims has just arrived,' Adam said in satisfaction. 'Thank you, Miss Blair. This is your resident security guard and breakfast-maker signing off. I'll see you tonight.'

Christy put the phone down and stared at the wall in stupefaction. What on earth had she done?

'I'm nuts,' she said aloud. 'I'm stark staring nuts.'

'I wouldn't say that, dear.' Christy pulled herself up short. An elderly lady had entered the pharmacy and was smiling up at her. 'I know the town thinks you're a little crazy, Miss Blair, but then the world needs a little craziness. And I need a repeat of my heart pills.'

Christy managed a laugh. 'You're right, of course, Miss Cotton. The world does need a little craziness. It's just that sometimes I take it to extremes.'

Christy's brother dropped into the shop while Christy was having her lunchtime sandwich. He walked in with the air of a man expecting to have things thrown at him. Christy looked down at her salad sandwich and longed to oblige. If the shop hadn't been vacuumed that morning. . .

'You're a brave man coming in here,' she told her brother direfully. 'Richard Blair, what are you doing to me?'

'I'm sorry, Christy.'

'You are not,' she told him. 'You're wearing an expression of a cat that's found the cream.'

'Kate slept all morning,' Richard told her, as if it made everything OK.

'Lucky Kate.'

'Christy, for heaven's sake. . .'

'I know, Christy said harshly. 'You need another doctor. Kate needs another doctor. Corrook needs another doctor. The only person round here who doesn't need another doctor is me, and I now have one. Whether I like it or not I have one making me an early morning cup of tea and toast and marmalade. . .'

'Did you accept him on that condition?' Richard asked, bemused.

'No. Yes.' Christy plonked down her half-eaten sandwich, grateful that the shop was empty apart from her and Richard. Ruth was off home for lunch and so, it seemed, were Christy's customers. 'Richard, what is Adam McCormack doing in Corrook?'

'I don't know.'

'Oh, come on,' she said, exasperated. 'You must know why he's decided to pick up his traps and move to Australia. His wife died six months ago, I gather.'

'I knew that.'

'Is that why he came? To get over her death?' She shook her head. 'Richard, you're wasting your time. Adam won't stay here. He's a city obstetrician, for heaven's sake. You should be advertising for a permanent partner.'

'Do you think I haven't tried?' Richard said wearily. 'You know the score, Christy. No one wants country practice. Adam's offer came in the nick of time as far as I'm concerned, and if he only stays for a week then it's still a bonus.' He fixed her with a stare. 'But he might. . .he just might stay a little longer if the locals are nice to him. And that includes you, Christy Blair.'

'I'm being nice to him,' Christy said bitterly. 'How much nicer can I be than offer to share my precious little cottage with him?'

'Offer?'

'OK, subject myself to being bludgeoned into sharing my cottage,' she conceded. 'But I did concede.' She managed a half-hearted smile. 'And I'll even take breakfast instead of rent, as long as the toast's hot.'

'You will be nice to him,' Richard said severely.

'I'll be nice to him. I'll be nice to him,' Christy repeated parrot fashion. 'What happened to his wife?'

'I don't know,' Richard told her. 'Adam hasn't told me and I haven't asked.'

'Richard!'

'It's none of my business, Christy.'

'Implying it's none of mine.' Christy eyed him dubiously. 'It seems to me I'm the last to know anything.' She hesitated. 'Richard, the first time I met Adam. . .the time you brought him home on leave. . .'

'Yes?'

'You told us Adam needed a break desperately. You told us he was caught up in some personal tragedy.

And you wouldn't tell us what it was. Did that have something to do with his marriage?'

'Christy, what you're asking isn't my right to tell,' Richard sighed. 'It's not ethical.'

'I'm not your patient here, Richard. I'm your sister. And I want to know.'

'Then you're just going to have to ask Adam,' Richard said firmly. 'Can I have a sandwich?'

'I've only one left.'

'I came to see you instead of going home to have lunch,' Richard said pathetically.

'More fool you. You should be home looking after Kate.'

'Matron was taking a quiche up to have lunch and a gossip with Kate.'

'So you elected to visit your sister instead,' Christy said slowly. 'Very kind of you, Richard.'

'Think nothing of it. Can I have the sandwich?'

'Oh, go right ahead,' she said bitterly. 'Feel free.' Then, as she saw him hesitate, she laughed. 'It's OK, Richard. I'm not hungry.'

'You're my favourite sister. Christy. . .'

Christy sighed. 'Now what?' she said resignedly.

He grinned. 'How did you guess I wanted something else?'

'It's getting to be a habit.'

'I have to go on a call out to Fred Barrow's after surgery.'

'You still need to do surgery? I thought after lending Adam the Mims he was set to take over.'

'Yeah, thanks for that.' Richard sighed. 'I should have thought. . .'

'You should have,' Christy said severely.

'Adam's spending the afternoon at the hospital getting to know the staff and making himself at home. I have a heavy surgery booked, and Fred lives ten miles out. It looks as if I won't be home until about seven.'

'So?'

'So, dear, kind Christy,' he grinned, 'I wonder if after you close up here you could drop in on Kate at around five-thirty?' His smile slipped. 'Matron's with her now but I don't like to leave her too long on her own.' His frown deepened. 'I don't think the baby's all that far away.'

'It's not due for two weeks.'

'I know.' He shook his head. 'I'm probably being over-anxious. She's agreed to have Adam examine her tomorrow morning and if he says so she'll go to Melbourne then. But until then. . .'

'I'll check on her.' Christy smiled and shook her head ruefully. 'It'll get me out of my house for a while longer.'

'Christy. . .'

'I know, I know,' she sighed. 'Be nice to Adam. I intend to be so saccharine-sweet to Adam that he won't be able to get back to London fast enough. I'll smile like the Cheshire cat. But I also will visit Kate. It'll give the Cheshire cat's face muscles a much needed break.'

'Thank you, Christy.' Still he hesitated.

'Now what?'

'Have you a spare house key? I'd like Adam to be able to settle himself in this afternoon.'

'Fine.' Christy struggled with her bunch of keys, tossing her spare to her brother. 'Tell him to make himself quite at home. The big bedroom's mine, but if it will make our Dr McCormack happier, then tell him to go right ahead and sleep in it. Anything else, big brother?'

Richard looked at her dubiously, and gave her what he clearly thought was an encouraging grin. 'Not that I'm game to ask,' he told her.

CHAPTER FOUR

FOR the remainder of Monday afternoon Christy was left in peace. It was just as well. The doctor's surgery was obviously busy with people eager to find out about the new doctor, and Christy had her hands full filling the resulting prescriptions. It was also hard work trying to read the scripts of a strange doctor.

'He's been educated in the standard practice of indecipherable doctor's handwriting,' she growled to Ruth. She peered at Adam's script. 'I don't think I've ever heard of this.'

'I told him he wasn't allowed to prescribe anything not in Mims,' Ruth said virtuously.

'That's a help.' Christy shrugged. Finally, nonplussed, she phoned the surgery.

'Have Dr McCormack spell out his requirement for Mrs Todd, will you, Bella?' she asked the receptionist.

'He's up at the hospital,' Bella said dubiously. 'He must have written that script this morning. Will you ring him there?'

'No.' The last thing Christy wanted was to talk to Adam. 'You contact him and ring me back.'

Two minutes later Bella was back on the line. She spelt the drug clearly and Christy bit her lip. It was clear once she knew. Once she was used to his writing she should have no problems.

'He said if you have any more queries to ring him at your place,' Bella said pleasantly. 'He's finished for the afternoon. He'll be home in twenty minutes, he said. He just had to do some shopping on the way home. Something about marmalade for his landlady?' There was a trace of laughter in Bella's voice.

'Fine,' Christy said and blushed like a schoolgirl. She

felt like one too. Gauche and out of her depth. Just as she'd been at twenty-one. . .

She filled her last script for the afternoon with relief, locked the shop and turned her little car in the direction of her brother's home. She glanced at her watch. Already it was after six and she'd promised Richard she'd check on Kate at five-thirty. Still, Richard was worrying unnecessarily. If Kate were his patient instead of his wife there would be no drama.

Kate and Richard lived just above the town in a big old farmhouse set back from the road. Christy pulled her little car into the garage under the house, and walked to the front door.

'Hi, Kate,' she called out as she approached the front door. The windows were wide open and Kate should hear her approaching. 'I'm here on guard duty, making sure you haven't dropped your bundle.'

There was no answer.

Christy frowned. The windows of the house were swung wide to let any breeze flow through to the rooms inside. The front door was hooked back, with only the screen door remaining closed.

'Kate?' she called again, and rang the bell.

Still nothing.

There were no cars around the house, but Richard would be driving his and Adam had Kate's. Maybe Kate had gone for a walk. Christy walked slowly around the house. Kate's little cat appeared from the back garden and wound herself around Christy's legs in greeting. Still no Kate. 'Kate?' Christy yelled, her brow creased in worry. Was she being stupid? She walked back up on to the veranda — and stopped dead. From inside the house came the faint mewing sound of. . .

Of a new-born baby. It had to be. There was no other sound like it. Christy's heart stopped beating. She must be imagining it.

'It's not due for two weeks,' she said out loud. 'It's

not. . .' She put her hand on the knob of the screen door and pulled. It was locked. From inside came the plaintive mewing once again. It wasn't imagination. Despite the late afternoon heat, Christy felt suddenly cold.

She wrenched hard at the screen door. It didn't move. 'Kate!' she yelled again and there was panic in her voice. Suddenly desperate, she brought back her sandalled foot and kicked as hard as she could. Her bare toes buckled under the pressure but the fly-wire screening tore inwards from the lower panel. Ignoring the pain in her foot, Christy bent down and scrambled through the ripped panel. 'Kate?' she screamed, struggling to her feet and running down the passage. 'Where are you, Kate? Kate!'

Then she stopped. She'd reached the door into the bathroom, and it was wide open, leading into the green-tiled floor beyond. There, huddled on the tiles, was Kate. At her thigh lay a squirming, blood-soaked bundle. The bundle writhed and cried again.

For a moment which would stay with Christy for the rest of her life, she thought Kate was dead. She bent down, scooping the babe to her and off the hard floor. The umbilical cord still held it to Kate. Christy laid a hand gently on Kate's neck. Her fingers felt a pulse.

'Oh, thank God,' she whispered. 'Thank God.' The pulse was definite, weak but steady.

Christy was crying in shock and fear. There was blood everywhere. Kate must have haemorrhaged to the point where she had lost consciousness.

The umbilical cord tying the baby to its mother meant that Christy couldn't move with the baby. She stared helplessly down. Should she cut the cord? Somewhere she'd read that you could bite it with your teeth. Rejecting the idea even as it came into her head, Christy grabbed a couple of thick towels from the shelf behind her, and wrapped the child firmly. She placed it gently down again on a pad of another towel against the unconscious Kate's thigh and ran for the phone.

Richard, she thought urgently. He's on the mobile. . . And then she stopped dead in her thoughts and gave a tiny sob of thankfulness. Richard would be miles away but Adam was here. Christy's cottage was the next house on this road and he should be home. She dialled her number with trembling fingers, barely able to make them work. Adam picked up the phone on the second ring.

'Adam?' she cut in before he could say anything.

'Miss Blair.' She could hear laughter in his voice. 'Ringing to check that I haven't pinched the big bed?'

'Adam, I'm. . . I'm at Kate's,' she said urgently, and suddenly she had all his attention.

'What's wrong?'

'She's. . .' Christy paused momentarily to get her voice working. 'Adam, she'd had the baby. She's. . . she's unconscious. There's blood. There's so much blood. . .'

'At home?'

'At home. On. . .on the floor. . .'

'Ring the ambulance,' Adam said curtly. 'Tell them to bring plasma. I'll be there in two minutes.' The line went dead.

He was there in less. Christy was back in the bathroom, staring helplessly down at Kate's limp form. She'd never seen so much blood. The baby stirred and Christy sat down and picked it up. Should she cut the umbilical cord? She hadn't a clue. Then she heard Adam's steps in the hall and could have wept with relief — could have if she weren't already weeping.

'In here,' she called out, and he was with her.

'My God.' Adam whistled silently. He was dressed in tailored trousers and a good quality linen shirt but his clothes were ignored. He placed his medical bag on the floor, knelt down in the blood and mess and reached for Kate's pulse.

'She's still alive,' Christy said dully. 'At least. . .at least I think so.'

'She is. You've called the ambulance?'

'Yes.'

Adam nodded. He washed fast at the handbasin, then knelt back on the floor. The baby first. As Christy unwrapped the blood-soaked bundle he cut the cord and tied it. The baby squawked its displeasure.

'At least we've no problems there,' Adam said grimly. 'Wrap him up again, Christy.' He was already bending over Kate, his fingers moving in a swift examination. 'Can you grab the ergometrine from my bag? Put his lordship back down on the towel. I need you.'

Seconds later the injection went home. Adam's face was grim. Once again he took Kate's pulse. What he felt obviously gave him no pleasure. Then a long, slow contraction rippled over the surface of Kate's belly and Adam's face lightened. 'It's coming now,' he said. His face was intent and grim. 'I think. . .'

A minute later he delivered the placenta. He held it up for a fast check of completeness and gave a low whistle of relief. 'That's more like it,' he said softly and placed it aside. 'The ergometrine will contract the uterus now,' he said. 'The bleeding should be slowing already.'

Christy had no way of telling. The floor was awash with blood and whether it was new or old she hadn't a clue. Adam was moving again, inserting a tube into Kate's arm and setting up a saline drip. Kate had been wearing a loose maternity frock, which allowed easy access to her arm. Not that it would matter if the dress had to be cut. Kate would in all likelihood never want to see the dress again.

If she survived. Christy stared down at Kate's blue-white face and suppressed a sob. Kate looked so far gone. Then the drip was up and Adam was moving back to check again.

'It has slowed,' he said softly. He took Kate's wrist.

'I think we were in time, Christy. The ergometrine's doing its job.' He glanced down at the still complaining baby. 'And we definitely have one healthy baby to show her when she comes to. There's nothing wrong with this little one.'

From outside came the sound of a siren, screaming up the hill towards them. 'You told them to bring plasma?' Adam asked and Christy nodded. She cradled the child to her in stunned silence, her eyes not leaving Kate's face. Adam said they were in time but Kate looked dreadful.

'Plasma's all we need to help her recover,' Adam told her gently. 'The bleeding's almost stopped. She'll make it, Christy.'

And then, as if to verify Adam's words, Kate stirred and opened her eyes.

'Well, well,' Adam said softly. He smiled down at Kate. 'Did you and Richard set this up to test your new partner?' he asked her. 'To see how Dr McCormack copes in a medical emergency?' Then at her look of dazed confusion he took her hand. 'You're fine, Kate,' he told her. 'You and Richard have a fine little boy. You have a very messy bathroom, but you have a son.' He motioned to Christy who placed the tiny towel-wrapped bundle next to Kate's face.

'Christy,' Kate said wonderingly in a thread of a voice. 'You're here.'

'I like blood and gore,' Christy said fondly. 'Where there's blood and gore, there's Christy Blair.' She smiled down at Kate, her tears drying on her cheeks as she saw the first faint tinge of colour return to her sister-in-law's cheeks. 'And I like my new little nephew.' Then she turned to Adam. 'Are you sure it's a nephew?' she demanded. 'I never noticed.'

Adam grinned, checking the drip in Kate's arm as he did. 'I've delivered hundreds of babies, ma'am, and I've never been wrong yet.'

'A son,' Kate whispered. 'Oh, Richard. . .' She closed her eyes and drifted again into oblivion.

'She's just exhausted,' Adam told Christy as he saw the panic start again in her eyes. Then the ambulance driver banged urgently on the front door and for a while Adam was occupied. With the plasma replacing saline as a drip, Kate was carefully loaded on to a stretcher and wheeled out to the waiting ambulance.

'You carry your nephew,' Adam told Christy. He looked down at the now sleeping bundle. 'It's lucky it was such a warm day. He doesn't seem chilled. In fact, he seems remarkably robust.'

'You're. . .you're not coming with us?' Christy said as an ambulance officer helped her into the back of the van. She looked up out at the blood-stained man standing behind the ambulance. With Adam, Kate was safe. With Adam she also could be safe. . . She looked down at the bundle in her arms and a tear slid down her cheek. If Adam hadn't been here. . .

'I'll follow you down in a moment,' Adam promised. He smiled in at her and reached up to trace the tear on her cheek with a finger. 'Kate's fine, Christy, and I have a call to make. Richard's carrying the mobile phone, and someone should tell him he has a son, don't you think?'

By the time the ambulance reached the hospital the plasma was starting to take effect on Kate. The blueness of her face had faded, and by the time she was safely tucked into bed she seemed to be in a natural sleep.

The shock was taking its toll on Christy. She was starting to believe she was almost as shocked as Kate. She stayed with her sister-in-law, holding Kate's hand as if she believed that in letting go Kate might slip away. Kate still seemed barely conscious but after examining her once more Adam assured Christy it was now just the aftermath of shock and exhaustion.

'Her blood-pressure's rising already,' he told her.

'By tomorrow she'll be sitting up in bed enjoying the drama.'

'Did you reach Richard?'

'Yes.' He sat down beside her in a chair at the bedside. 'He'll be here as soon as he can.'

'He shouldn't have left her,' Christy said bitterly.

Adam shook his head. 'He couldn't have anticipated this,' he said firmly. 'He did what he could by asking you to check. And Matron was there at lunchtime. . .'

'I certainly was.' The lady in question bustled disapprovingly into the room. 'I can't believe this happened. Kate looked uncomfortable at lunchtime, but she ate the quiche I took her and assured me she was fine when I left at two. Then four hours later this happened.'

Kate opened her eyes wearily. 'Sorry, Alma,' she told Matron, her voice faint and far-away. 'I was trying to be clever.'

'Clever,' Alma snorted. 'I suppose that means you knew you were in labour at lunchtime.'

'I was having contractions,' Kate admitted. 'But they were so far apart. I knew if I told Richard he'd fuss, and it was Adam's first day. . . I thought if I could wait until Richard came home tonight then he could take me to hospital. But then. . .but then everything happened so fast. I thought my waters had broken, but the baby came and there was so much blood. . . And I couldn't get to the phone. . .'

'It's OK, Kate,' Adam told her gently. 'Christy coped brilliantly. She can take up a second calling as midwife.'

'No chance,' Christy said soundly. 'You've put me off motherhood for good. If I can't find a baby under a cabbage leaf then I'm destined to be an aunt and only an aunt forever. Speaking of my nephew. . .' From the nursery next door came a lusty wail and Christy managed a smile. 'Is that him?'

'We put him in a humidicrib to get his body tempera-

ture up a bit,' Adam told her. 'It's a precaution only,
but he doesn't need it and he doesn't want it.' He
smiled down at Kate. 'He wants his mum. Does his
mum want him?'

'Yes, please,' Kate whispered. 'Adam. . .' And then
her voice faltered. From the corridor outside came the
sound of Richard's voice, raised in harsh, anxious
interrogation. A nurse answered and then Richard was
at the door. He had eyes only for Kate.

Christy gently disengaged her hand from Kate's and
stood up. Her body was stiff and tired. Adam glanced
at Richard, down at Kate, and then took Christy's arm.

'I don't think we're needed any more,' he told
Christy. 'Let's go home.'

They had to pass Kate's and Richard's home on the
way back to Christy's cottage. Adam slowed as they
neared the house, sped up again and then reluctantly
took his foot off the accelerator. He swung his car into
Richard's driveway, where Christy's little car was
parked.

'You're not thinking what I'm thinking?' he said
grimly.

Christy wrinkled her nose. 'Richard's so tired
already. I can't let him come home to this mess.' She
took a deep breath. 'You go on,' she told Adam. 'I can
do this, then I'll drive myself home.' To reinforce her
intention, she pointedly fished her car keys out of her
bag.

'I didn't think blood was your favourite substance,'
Adam smiled and Christy grimaced further. She visibly
squared her shoulders and stood up out of the car. She
winced as the weight went down on the foot she'd used
to kick in the screen door. She'd hardly noticed it
before but it was starting to hurt now.

'I'll cope,' she told Adam. 'Kate's my sister-in-law
and Richard's my brother. This is something I
have to do.'

'Thus spake the martyr.'

'I don't have to enjoy it,' Christy snapped. But I have to do it. Go home, Dr McCormack.'

Adam looked down at his stained clothes and shook his head. 'It seems a pity to waste these filthy clothes.' He smiled down at Christy and her heart twisted. The creases at the corners of his eyes — his laugh-lines — transformed his face when he smiled and Christy could barely take her eyes off him. 'You go home,' he told her. 'Heat up some baked beans for dinner while I do this,' he offered.

'We don't have baked beans,' Christy said involuntarily.

'Yes, we do. I bought 'em today.'

'But I'm having sausages for dinner.' She was being inane, but she was thrown right off balance.

'Sausages?' His smile deepened. 'Baked beans and sausages are my favourite.'

'I only have two sausages.'

'I was willing to share my baked beans,' he said, injured. 'Two divides into halves really well.'

Christy saw domestic harmony yawning before her. Shared house. Shared meals. . . She was tired, she was confused and she was past being polite.

'Oh, go home,' she snapped. 'Leave me to clean here. I'll cook my own dinner when I get home.'

Adam shook his head. With a deft movement he lifted her car keys from her hand and dropped them provocatively down the front of his shirt. His smile turned wicked and he undid the second button of his shirt. His hard, muscled chest showed, with blond-brown hairs against the light weave of his cotton shirt. 'Unless you'd like to fetch them, they stay there until the house is cleaned,' he tested.

Christy drew in her breath on an indignant gasp. She turned on her heels and stalked into the house, ignoring the pain in her foot. Adam chuckled low in his throat and followed her in.

By the time the cleaning was done Christy was exhausted. She felt emotionally drained and rather sick.

It was as well Adam had helped her, she admitted to herself. Such a job would have made her physically ill if she'd tackled it alone. Still, at least there was a happy outcome. How much worse would the job have been if Kate or the baby—or both—had died?

'Thank you,' she said stiffly as they put the last of the cleaning materials away.

'I don't believe what I'm hearing,' Adam smiled. He touched her cheek with a finger and Christy flinched. 'You mean you're actually feeling something for me other than blatant dislike?'

'I'm feeling grateful,' Christy snapped. 'And I'm also feeling dead tired. I need my dinner and my bed.'

'And so say all of us,' Adam agreed fervently. 'You'll be pleased to know I didn't take your big bedroom. Though your bed does look much more comfortable than the single in the back room,' he said plaintively.

'I suppose you checked,' Christy said, before she could help herself.

'Of course,' Adam told her. 'I went through the entire house. I've checked the state of the windowsills for dust. I've inspected the bottom reaches of your knicker drawer, counted the holes in your socks and I've read every one of the four hundred and fifty-three love letters you keep tied up with pink string in the bottom of your bureau.' He stooped down and picked up Kate's little cat, which was purring around his stained trouser leg. 'Do you think we should feet her?'

'I'll do it,' Christy said stiffly. 'You can go home.'

Christy watched the little cat eat her supper while her bright red cheeks slowly faded to her normal colour. Adam McCormack spent his time laughing at her. Adam McCormack could go to hell.

She emerged from the kitchen to find Adam had left already, running her car out on to the road. Her keys were on the front door step. For long moments she stood on the veranda, trying to find the courage to go on. To find the courage to climb into the little car and go home. To go home to Adam. . .

Adam was cooking as she came in. He'd changed into jeans and a dark checked shirt, and had scrubbed away the last traces of Kate's blood. Sausages were frying in the pan, a saucepan of baked beans bubbled beside it and a bowl of salad sat invitingly on Christy's table.

'You've moved fast,' Christy said grudgingly.

'I move fastest when I'm hungry,' he told her. He held an egg up. 'One or two?'

'One, thanks,' she said automatically.

'I cook my eggs for four minutes,' Adam warned her. 'Four-minute shower, ma'am.'

'Yes, sir.' Her rejoinder was automatic. The fire had gone out of her. She was too tired to argue.

It was slightly more than four minutes before she re-emerged. This time last night she would have flinched at the idea of appearing before Adam McCormack in her flimsy housecoat, with her blond hair streaming damply down her back. Now she was too tired to care. If Adam hadn't been here she would have fallen straight into bed without eating. Now. . . Adam was serving plates of food as though he belonged here — as if his rightful place was in her kitchen.

She hardly ate. Adam's presence disconcerted her, and the events of the past few hours had spoilt what little appetite she would otherwise have had. She made a half-hearted attempt to eat, but finally she rose from the table. After twenty minutes of being still, her injured foot had stiffened and now pain shot through her leg in a savage jab. She bit back a gasp of pain and took her plate to the sink. Adam rose as well.

'You don't like baked beans?' he asked, gently taking her plate from her.

'I'm just not hungry,' she told him. She was shivering. Maybe it was reaction to the drama of the evening, or maybe it was the presence of this man so close to her. She caught her breath. 'I. . .it wasn't the beans. I didn't eat my sausage either.'

'I don't blame you,' Adam said. 'Sausages and baked beans aren't my ideal food. If I were in London now I'd whisk you out to an intimate French restaurant and show you what food can really be.'

You did that once before, Christy thought dully.

'Christy, Kate really is OK,' Adam told her, misinterpreting the look on her face.

'I know.'

'So what. . .?'

'I'm just tired,' Christy snapped. She tried to push past him but, standing between the table and the bench, Adam effectively blocked her path. 'Dr McCormack, I need to go to bed. I didn't sleep well last night. I've had an awful day and I have a big day tomorrow. Will you let me past, please?'

'Why didn't you sleep last night?' Adam asked.

'It's none of your business.' Christy bit her lip despairingly. 'Please,' she said weakly, 'please, will you just let me be?'

He was frowning down at her as if what she was saying were totally incomprehensible. 'Christy, what have I done to you to make you so upset?' He took her shoulders in his hands and forced her to meet his look. 'I don't have a clue what's going on here.'

'Neither do I.' Christy was close to tears. She thrust her hands up to break his grip on her shoulders and pushed past him. He made no move to stop her. 'Goodnight, Dr McCormack.'

'You're limping.'

Christy had reached the door. She pulled it open. 'Goodnight,' she said definitely.

'But——'

'I can limp if I want to,' she said desperately. 'Leave me alone.'

* * *

Exhaustion made Christy sleep for about two hours. After that the pain in her foot woke her.

Her foot seemed on fire. It was burning hot and throbbing in shards of pain that made her want to weep. The weight of the light sheet she had thrown over herself seemed unbearable.

She lay and stared into her moonlit room, willing the pain to ease. The chirk-chirk of the nightjar hunting insects in the bush beyond the house normally soothed and comforted her when she was troubled. Tonight it seemed almost mocking. Life goes on, it was saying. Your world falls apart but the rest of the world couldn't give a damn.

Christy wiped a tear away from her cheek in anger. She was being crazy. She was acting like a stupid, lovestruck adolescent all over again. Why couldn't she act like a rational human being while Adam was around?

Adam would by now be soundly asleep. Why was she lying in bed? There was aspirin in the kitchen cupboard. It was fear of seeing Adam that was keeping her in bed, and that fear was crazy. She threw the sheet from her body and swung her feet on to the floor.

The pain in her foot made her cry out. She bit back the exclamation and closed her eyes, willing the jabbing thrusts to ease. There was a chair beside her bed. Holding it before her, she pushed her way to the door. The chair made a scraping sound on the bare, polished boards of the floor but Adam's room was at the rear of the cottage. This much noise wouldn't disturb him.

By the time she reached the kitchen she was no longer using the chair for support, the pain easing slightly as she forced her ankle into use. It's just badly bruised, she told herself thankfully, pouring herself a glass of water and searching in the cupboard above the sink for the aspirin. A couple of tablets. . .

'It won't work.'

Adam's soft voice behind her made her jump. When she came down to earth she'd shifted her weight to her bad foot again and she had to clutch the sink for support. Then Adam flicked on the light behind her. She turned reluctantly to face him.

He was wearing cotton pyjama trousers and nothing more. His sandy hair was tousled by sleep and the muscles of his chest were clearly delineated. It was as much as Christy could do not to gasp again. She put her hands behind her, still needing the support of the sink.

'Aspirin's not strong enough,' he told her, coming into the room. 'If your foot's hurting, I'll give you something more effective.'

'My foot's fine.'

'You make a lousy liar.' Adam had reached her now. Stooping, he bent to look, and then whistled as he saw the bruising around the ankle, and the laceration on her big toe. 'Christy, for heaven's sake. How did this happen?'

'I kicked in Kate's door,' she said sullenly. She was behaving like an ungracious brat and she knew it. 'I. . . I'm sorry I woke you.'

'I was awake, anyway,' he told her. 'I want to phone England. It's mid-morning over there and I've promised someone I'll ring. I assumed it would be OK with you if I used the phone. I'll certainly have any calls costed and pay for them.'

'Oh.' Christy's anger was suddenly replaced by desolation. Adam McCormack still had a life she knew nothing about. A tragedy. . .a wife. . .maybe another woman. . . She slumped down on to a chair, weary beyond belief. 'Ring whoever you like' she said dully.

'Let me see your foot,' Adam insisted. Still kneeling, his cool, firm fingers probed her burning flesh. The feel of his fingers made her want to cringe but she made herself stay still. Finally he stopped.

'The ankle just seems to be twisted,' he told her. 'Not too badly, either, or you wouldn't have been able to walk afterwards. It's using it so much afterwards that's made it hurt now. If you'd let me clean. . .' He sighed. 'You've broken this toe, though, Christy. I think it's a clean fracture of the phalanx. I'll get an X-ray tomorrow morning, but I'm ninety per cent sure that's what you've done.'

'Oh,' she said blankly. She shook her head, fighting off visions of lumps of plaster dangling from her big toe.

'If I'm right you won't need plaster,' Adam told her, guessing her thoughts. 'Just closed-in shoes to protect it. I'll get my bag and give you an injection to let you sleep.'

'I don't need an injection.'

'You'll live without one,' he agreed. 'But a shot of morphine will give you a good night's sleep and, as I'm your prescribing doctor, that's what you stand in need of more than anything. Now, are you intent on martyrdom, or can I give you an injection?'

Christy shook her head again, and then nodded. She was being stupid. She was dead tired and her foot hurt so much it made her want to cry. Or was it the foot?

'OK,' she said wearily, and then, realising how ungracious she must sound, she managed a smile. 'Thank you, Dr McCormack.'

'Adam,' he said gently.

'Adam.'

He touched her face. 'First things first, then, Christy Blair. Let's get you back to bed.' Before she realised what he intended he scooped her up into his arms. Christy gave an indignant gasp.

'Put me down.'

'I thought we'd agreed to end the martyrdom,' he said, ignoring her demand. He pushed open the kitchen door with his foot and strode easily through the house to her bedroom. His arms held her firmly to his hard body. Christy's thin nightgown was no barrier between her skin and the hard maleness of Adam's bare chest. Her body curled against him as though it had found a home and Christy couldn't suppress a shudder. This was where she wanted to be more than anything else in the world, and yet to want this was crazy. Finally Adam laid her carfully on her bed and stood back. 'Not so bad, now, was it, Miss Blair?'

'I. . . Thank you,' she muttered.

'Will you need bedclothes? I can use a couple of kitchen chairs to set up a cradle over your foot.'

'I don't need a cradle,' she said abruptly, and then tempered her tone. 'I. . . It's warm enough to go without bedclothes.'

He nodded and left. Two minutes later he was back with an injection. 'Relax,' he told her. 'This won't hurt a bit.'

'That's what they all say.'

Adam grinned. 'Oh, ye of little faith. . .' The needle slid painlessly home and was withdrawn. 'Now what have you to say, Miss Blair?'

'Lucky shot,' she said.

'Unfair.'

Christy managed a weak smile. 'I know,' she admitted. 'I'm sorry.'

For a long moment he stood looking down at the girl on the bed. Her tangled blonde curls were spread out on the pillow. The thin fabric of her nightgown clung revealingly to the soft curves of her body. Adam McCormack thought her lovely and his eyes showed it.

'Are you this scratchy with every male, or just with me?' Adam asked softly. Then, as she drew in her breath, he put a finger on her mouth to stop her answering. 'Maybe I don't want to know,' he said. 'But Christy, I'd keep the defences up if I were you. Something tells me you're going to need them.'

'Don't be ridiculous,' she muttered. 'And get out of my room.

'Are you sure you want me to?'

'Adam. . .'

There was a long silence. It stretched on and on. Adam was looking down in the moonlight and the look on his face showed Christy that he was as confused and torn as she.

'Adam. . .'

Then, very slowly, Adam bent and softly kissed her. His finger on her lips was replaced by his mouth.

It was nothing like the kiss she remembered. Last time Adam McCormack had kissed her, his lips had burned into hers. They had been hard, demanding and unyielding. She had thought it was a kiss of desire — a kiss claiming her as his woman — and she had been horribly, cruelly wrong. This kiss, though, was a question. His lips brushed hers with no pressure at all.

And then he was gone. Her bedside lamp was turned off and the door of the bedroom closed gently behind him.

Christy was left staring into the dark, her lips warm where he had touched. She put a finger up as if to keep the feel of him with her. This was not the Adam she remembered. This, though. . .this was an Adam whom she could fall in love with all over again, as if five years ago had never happened. The image she had been carrying in her heart for the last five years was changing, but it still held her heart in its grip.

And then she heard the phone come off the receiver and Adam talking softly so as not to disturb her. 'London, please, operator.'

Christy shook her head into the dark. It was no business of hers whom Adam phoned. She didn't want to know. She didn't. . .

'Helen? It's Adam. May I speak to Fiona, please?'

There was a pause and when Adam spoke again his voice had softened to a point Christy hardly recognised.

'Fi, love. How are you, sweetheart? Missing me?'

Christy could bear no more. She pulled her pillow

from under her head and buried her face in it, muffling the sounds from the other room. Damn Adam McCormack. Damn him, damn him, damn him.

She closed her eyes and willed sleep to come. After a while the morphine took hold, and she drifted into oblivion.

CHAPTER FIVE

CHRISTY woke as the morphine wore off, just before dawn. She lay and stared into the dimly lit room, listening to the dawn chorus from the trees around the house. The birds were welcoming the day with joy. Why couldn't she?

She had a new nephew. She remembered the existence of a new person in her life with a smile. This baby would be special. Maybe this new baby would help her get over this stupid, stupid crush.

'I'm going mad,' she said to the ceiling. 'It's not logical to feel like this about someone. I'm like the lady in *Great Expectations*, sitting in her wedding gown fifty years later.'

She sat up with a jolt, swearing softly as she jarred her foot. There was no way she was going to be like that. She'd show Adam McCormack she could be totally oblivious to his insidious smile. She'd show him. A new day. A new life. A new Christy. Adam McCormack would be treated as a friend from this moment forth.

She showered with difficulty, dragging a stool into the recess so that she could sit down while she washed, and then dressed with care. By the time she appeared in the kitchen the sun was well up and the dawn chorus was long since past. There was no sign of Adam. 'So much for my promised breakfast in bed,' she muttered, and then frowned. Adam had taken care of her foot in the night. It was unfair of her to expect more. On the window-ledge perched a rather rotund kookaburra, eyeing her hopefully. Christy laughed at his quizzical expression.

'Bacon's only served on Sunday,' she told him firmly, then relented. She found a remnant of cold sausage,

opened the window, and her offering was accepted
with dignity.

'And that's all,' she said firmly. 'You're getting fat,
Charlie. Go and catch your own meals.' She paused as
the stillness was broken. There was a car coming up
the hill towards her cottage. A moment later, the
hospital car swung into the drive. Adam.

She'd assumed he was still in bed. Some optimistic
expectation of being gone before he rose had driven
her to rise early. It hadn't worked. Adam must have
been awake long before her.

He came quietly into the back porch, closing the
door carefully behind him to prevent it banging, and
then stopped dead when he saw her.

'Well, well.' He looked tired, but his eyes creased
into a smile. 'I thought you wouldn't be up until you'd
been given your tea and toast.'

'I waited for hours,' she said plaintively. She looked
pointedly at her watch. The time was just seven-thirty.
'I'm usually up hours before this.'

He chuckled. 'I don't believe it.' He crossed to the
stove.

'There's coffee percolating,' Christy offered.

'You're a woman in a million.' He frowned. 'I
thought you only liked tea.'

'I was just being difficult,' Christy admitted, sticking
hard to her resolution. She was going to act cheerful if
it killed her.

He raised his eyebrows and said nothing.

Christy sighed. 'Adam, I have been unfair,' she said
slowly. She forced herself to meet his eyes. This man
had a woman in England. Hostility would do nothing
but make them both miserable. She searched in her
mind for an excuse and found one ready-made. 'I've
been worried sick about Kate.'

'There was no need.'

Christy hesitated. 'You. . .you weren't called out to
Kate again? Is that why you were out?'

'I was,' Adam admitted. 'Kate's running a slight fever, but I think it's insignificant at this stage.' He looked hard at her. 'So you were grumpy because you were frightened?'

Christy shrugged and carried the percolator carefully to the table, avoiding putting weight on her bad foot. 'The thought of childbirth leaves me cold,' she lied. 'What happened yesterday just confirms what I've always felt. Aunt is as close to motherhood as I'll ever get.'

'Maybe you should plan to adopt,' Adam said lightly. 'Or marry a widower with children.'

Christy shook her head. 'Domestic harmony's not for the likes of me. I'm out for a good time.'

'Forever?' Adam sounded startled.

'Forever,' she said firmly. She sat down hard.

Adam was silent for a moment, frowning into the distance. He reached for the percolator and poured coffee, then sat for a while before talking again. Finally as Christy rose he seemed to come out of his reverie. 'Foot's still bad?'

'Yes.'

'Let me see.'

Christy obligingly held it out before her. She had dressed in a light, cotton dress but left her feet bare until now, unsure how best to protect the injury.

Adam's fingers ran lightly over the bruised flesh, noting that the swelling of her ankle had already subsided a little with the night's rest. He smiled up at her but Christy was staring fixedly ahead. To Adam it seemed as if she was being stoic in pain. What he didn't know was that the pain didn't come from her ankle.

'I'll wrap the ankle to support it,' he said. 'Have you any closed-in shoes that are loose enough to go over a dressing?'

'I've some white moccasins,' Christy said dubiously. 'They'll look strange.'

'Less strange than plaster, which is the alternative. Protect that toe or else.'

'Yes, sir,' she muttered.

He grinned. 'That's better,' he approved. He'd brought his bag in with him, and for a few moments concentrated on wrapping her foot securely. As the foot was supported, the pain decreased accordingly.

'You'd do well to stay off your foot for the day,' Adam told her.

'I'll sit in the dispensary,' she promised.

'That's not what I meant. Your foot should be up.'

'If Ruth fetches and carries, then I can sit in state filling prescriptions.'

Adam nodded reluctantly. 'It's not ideal, but I guess it's the best you can do.' He sighed. 'It seems you're almost as indispensable to this town as Richard.'

Christy shook her head. 'Richard has Kate, and now he has you,' she said softly. 'There's no one to take over the pharmacy if I'm not available.'

Adam looked down at her. 'You're carrying a fair responsibility for a. . .' He stopped.

'For a kid?' Christy finished for him.

Adam smiled. 'I was going to say that,' he admitted. 'You don't seem very old.'

'Richard's little sister,' Christy said, her voice suddenly bleak. She stood painfully and moved to the door. 'I'll leave you to your breakfast while I find my moccasins.'

'Christy?'

She paused and looked back. 'What?'

Adam frowned. 'Christy, I didn't mean to hurt you,' he said as if he hardly knew whether he'd done so, but was aware by the change in her tone that he'd said something wrong.

Christy shrugged and managed a smile. Being called a kid by anyone other than Adam McCormack wouldn't worry her in the least.

'Just keep calling me a kid,' she said softly. 'By the time I'm forty I'll be grateful for it.'

Her next trial was her car. She limped from the house to the car and started the engine. Then she tried putting her foot on the clutch. Her foot told her that whwat she was doing was a really stupid idea.

'But I drove you last night,' she told her little car in dismay. 'I could do it then.'

'Your foot's stiffened.' Adam had followed her out of the house and was standing on the veranda holding coffee in one hand and toast in the other.

Christy swore and tried again. Her foot stabbed her painfully. Reluctantly she withdrew.

'I'll ring for Pete's taxi,' she told Adam. She was trying hard not to look at him. In his light trousers and checked, short-sleeved shirt, and with his coffee and toast, he looked as if he belonged to the place. Domestic harmony, Christy thought savagely and limped forward.

'I'll drive you.' Adam glanced at his watch. 'Why so early?'

'I want to do some bookwork before the shop opens,' she told him.

'The book work can wait. You need an X-ray and a pair of crutches before you go to work. Give me ten minutes to shower and change and I'll drive you down.'

Christy nodded. There was nothing else she could do. She was growing more indebted to this man and she didn't like it one bit. The alternative, though — well, there was no alternative.

Half an hour later, suitably fitted with crutches, she limped into her sister-in-law's ward at the hospital. Adam was doing rounds with Richard and there was time to kill. 'I'm starting surgery at nine,' Adam had told her. 'Wait here and I'll take you to the pharmacy on the way.'

'Fine,' Christy agreed. She was getting quite good at

agreeing, she thought ruefully. Adam McCormack was a man used to leadership, and he assumed Christy was happy to follow. So follow she did. But not happily.

Kate was propped up with a mountain of pillows, cradling her infant son. She looked up in delight as Christy appeared and then frowned as she saw the crutches.

'What on earth have you done?'

'I had an argument with a rock,' Christy said blandly. She limped over to look down at the baby. 'So this is what the fuss was all about. What are you naming him?'

'Andrew James. Christy. . .?'

'That's a fine name,' Christy approved and sat down. 'Is he feeding well?'

Kate was not so easily side-tracked. She shifted her sleeping son to the cot beside the bed and fixed Christy with a look. 'How did you hurt your foot?'

'Kicking Dr McCormack?' Christy tried.

Kate smiled. 'I gather you'd like to.'

'Dr McCormack is a very estimable medical practitioner,' Christy said mechanically. She relented and smiled. 'I'm very grateful to him, Kate.'

'Aren't we all,' Kate sighed. She put the covers over her infant son with one hand, her other hand continuing to rest against his cheek. 'He gave me Andrew.'

'He did not,' Christy retorted. 'Adam might have stopped you bleeding, but your son was doing fine all by himself. He was squawking his lungs out at his mistreatment while his mum was bleeding to death. It's my belief if I hadn't come he would have cut the cord himself and hiked into the kitchen for a feed.'

Kate chuckled. She gave her son an affectionate pat and turned again to Christy. 'So you hurt your foot how?'

'I told you,' Christy said firmly. 'A rock or Adam. Take your pick.'

'It wouldn't have anything to do with the ruddy great

hole in our fly-screen door?' a voice demanded, and the girls turned to the door. Richard had come into the room, and behind him was Adam.

'Your son did that,' Christy told Richard. 'The ambulance driver offered to open it, but your macho baby just flew in, boots and all.'

Richard shook his head and turned to Adam. 'Has she let you see it?'

'The door?' Adam asked. He ducked as one of Kate's pillows came hurtling across the room at him. He grinned down at Kate. 'Feeling better, then?'

'Can I take my drip out?'

'After twenty-four hours,' he told her firmly. He picked up her chart. 'I'm glad to see you're controlling your temperature, Mrs Blair. Keep up the good work.' He looked at Christy. 'Ready to go?'

'But what's wrong with Christy's foot?' Kate wailed. 'Adam, you can't take her without telling us.'

Adam shook his head. 'It's not a pretty story,' he said sagely. 'You'd be shocked, Kate. I'd tell Richard but I've taken an oath in regard to patient confidentiality. Christy and her rock can take their stories to the grave, in the knowledge that I'll never let out their dreadful secret.'

They left them laughing, and Christy chuckled as Adam helped her out to the car. He assisted her in and then stood, looking curiously down at her.

'Why don't you do that more often?' he asked.

'What?'

'Laugh.' He picked up her crutches and threw them into the back seat. 'I get the feeling life is a pretty serious business for Christy Blair.'

Only since you came, she thought. She didn't say it, though. Instead she shook her head.

'I told you. I've been worried.'

'So from here on in life is fun again.'

Christy eyed him cautiously as he lowered himself into the driver's seat. 'I suppose so,' she said dubiously.

'Good.' He grinned across at her. 'We'll start tonight, then.'

'Tonight?'

'I'm not much for baked beans. I have a hell of a day's work ahead of me and by the time you get home you won't be up to cooking either. We'll eat in style tonight.'

'I don't. . . I don't think Corrook is set up for dining in style.'

'It has a pub.'

'Oh.' Christy smiled.

'What do you mean, "oh"?'

Christy's smile deepened. 'I can see how some people think formica tables, the smell of stale beer and a plate of steak and chips is "style",' she said softly. 'How bad are things on the National Health at home?'

He grinned. 'As soon as Kate's on her feet and able to give anaesthetic back-up for Richard again I'll show you just what style really is, my lady. Even if I have to fly you to London to do it.'

Christy flicked back her curls in a mock-imperious gesture. 'There's no need,' she assured him. 'I know exactly what style is.' She lowered her voice to a hushed, awed voice. 'I've been inside the Corrook Café!'

Adam shook his head in wonder. 'Well,' he said. 'What more can I say? I suppose I couldn't stun you with the fact that my aunty's best friend's nephew is practically sure his dog is related to one of the Queen's corgis?'

'I am unstunnable,' Christy said grandly. And then spoiled the effect entirely by chuckling.

They were still laughing when they pulled up outside the pharmacy. Adam retrieved her crutches and then assisted her from the car, watched by a goggle-eyed Ruth.

'I'll see you tonight, then,' Adam told her firmly, as she withdrew her arm from his, took her crutches and adjusted the balance. He frowned. 'I doubt if I can get away at five-thirty to take you home.'

'I'll use a taxi,' Christy assured him. 'Thank you, Dr McCormack.'

He grinned. 'A bit of formality is OK because of the corgis,' he told her kindly. 'But for someone who's seen the inside of the Corrook Café. . . Well, it's quite proper to call me Adam.' He paused reflectively. 'Or just McCormack, really. If you really have been inside. . .'

Christy shook her head, still laughing. 'Thank you, Adam,' she told him.

'Think nothing of it. I'll pick you up at home at seven, or as near to it as I can manage.' Then, before Christy knew what he intended, he lifted a finger to his lips and transferred it to hers. 'Look after your toe, Christy, love.'

And he was gone.

'Miss Blair. . .' Ruth breathed. She was standing on the pavement staring after him in awe. 'Oh, Miss Blair. Oh, he's lovely.'

Christy was taking one deep breath after another. It was just as well Ruth wasn't looking at her, because she was the colour of fire. Finally she came back to earth.

'It's ten past nine, Ruth,' she managed. 'And the shop's still locked.'

'It can stay locked,' Ruth sighed. 'Oh, lucky you, Miss Blair.'

'Lucky me?'

'For having a sore toe,' Ruth explained patiently. 'I think I can feel a whole epidemic of them coming on.'

It took Christy nearly half an hour to achieve some sort of normal routine. Her world seemed to be turned upside-down. The Christy who had left the shop yesterday was not the one who had returned to it this morning.

Maybe I should continue to be nasty to him, she told herself. It's less dangerous. If he kept smiling. . . It was his smile she had fallen in love with, that and his ability to make her laugh when things seemed at their blackest.

He's a friend now, she told herself harshly. I have to learn to enjoy him as a friend. She touched her lips where his finger had touched. Dr McCormack was a warm and sensual person. Such a gesture to him meant nothing more than friendship. She knew that now from bitter experience.

'So get on with your life,' she said aloud, grimly, adjusting her typewriter spool. The row of sticky labels waiting to be typed on had twisted. She finally got it right and started.

    Mrs M. Haddon,
    Valium. . .

She stopped typing and frowned. Reaching for a card index, she flipped it open until she found what she wanted. She stared down at the card file. There had been a prescription for Valium filled last Thursday and before that three weeks ago. And the script of three weeks ago was written by a different doctor than this one. Both doctors were from out of town. Christy hadn't heard of either.

'Mrs Haddon?'

A middle-aged lady looked up from where she had been browsing in the cosmetics. She smiled at Christy.

'Hi, love,' she beamed. Like most of Corrook's population, Mrs Haddon knew and was fond of the young pharmacist. She had been an early friend of Christy's. Without family in the town she often popped into the pharmacy to have a chat with Christy and Ruth.

Christy sighed, picked up her crutches and came around so that she could talk to the lady without Ruth hearing.

'Mr Haddon, didn't I fill a Valium prescription for you last Thursday?'

Mrs Haddon nodded. Was it Christy's imagination or had her gaze shifted slightly away, so that she wasn't quite meeting Christy's look? 'You did, dear,' she admitted. 'But I'm that forgetful. I must have thrown the packet into the rubbish with my supermarket bags. What have you done to your foot?'

'You didn't use any of the last script?' Christy asked, refusing to be side-tracked.

'Oh, no, dear,' Mrs Haddon said, shocked. 'I couldn't use all those tablets without going silly in the head. I lost them, like I said. Now, tell me about your foot. And have you met your new little nephew yet? I hear he's just like his dad. I've made a casserole for Dr Blair, and I'm taking it around this afternoon. I've knitted a little jacket too. All I have to do now is thread it with blue ribbon.'

Christy gave up and retired, only half satisfied. A niggle of doubt remained. The script she was filling was a repeat, so she had no grounds to refuse to fill it. She stared down at it unhappily. It was written by a doctor who practised in Tynong, the next town, forty miles away. What was Mrs Haddon doing going there for treatment, and, if she did, why get her scripts filled here?

There was probably a reason. Maybe she didn't like Richard, and until this week there had only been Richard, or the increasingly unavailable Kate. Still. . .

She made out the script, waited until Mrs Haddon left the shop and then phoned the pharmacy in Tynong.

Two minutes later she was feeling even more disturbed.

'She won't have lost the script,' Rob, the chemist at Tynong, said definitely. 'She's brought in three different scripts from as many doctors in the last couple of months and repeats as well. I gave her a hard time last week when she brought in a script from a doctor I'd never heard of. So she's come back to you.'

Kate looked down at the copy of the script in her hand. 'Do you know a Dr Cartwright?'

'Nope.'

'It says here he's from Tynong.'

There was a moment's silence. When Rob spoke again his voice had changed from casual interest to worry.

'There was a doctor here called Dr Cartwright,' he said. 'I'd forgotten him. He came here nearly eighteen months ago as assistant with a view to join the medical partnership. He left after three days.'

Christy drew in her breath. 'How on earth. . .?'

'Christy, there's been a couple of break-ins at the Tynong surgery over the last few months. Cartwright's script pads may not have been destroyed. The two doctors here now reported their script pads stolen but they might have overlooked Cartwright's.'

'Oh.'

'You've a problem, Christy,' her associate told her firmly. 'You're going to have to report this to the police.'

'I know,' Christy said unhappily. She shook her head at the phone. 'I can't see Mrs Haddon breaking into a surgery.'

'She wouldn't have to,' the chemist told her. 'Often stolen script pads are sold, and sold for a hell of a lot of money.'

'But how on earth. . .?'

'Christy, I've a queue of five customers,' Rob told her. 'It's a matter for the police now.'

'I know.'

She put the phone down, but then stood staring at the instrument until Ruth came back into the dispensary and asked if her foot was hurting.

'No.' Christy shook her head. Mrs Haddon was a

kindly middle-aged matron who had clucked over her since her arrival in Corrook. This seemed so wrong.

Ruth put her head to one side. 'Thinking about Dr McCormack?'

'Why would I be thinking of Dr McCormack?' Christy demanded, and Ruth giggled.

'Just thought I'd ask, Miss Blair,' she said, grinning. She gestured out to the shop front. 'Mr Harris is here for his tablets.'

Christy nodded. 'Can you ring the surgery and ask Dr Blair or Dr McCormack if I can speak to them?'

Ruth nodded, still grinning. 'I'll ask for Dr McCormack first, shall I?'

Christy raised a crutch. 'You see this, Ruth?'

Ruth giggled and picked up the phone. 'I don't know what the Workers' Compensation Board would say to me being brained with a crutch, Miss Blair.'

'They'd say it was justifiable homicide,' Christy said shortly.

Regardless of who Ruth asked for, it was Adam who was available. As Ruth took Mr Harris's tablets down into the shop, Christy picked up the phone.

'What's wrong, Christy?' Adam sounded busy and harrassed.

'Is Richard there?'

'He's up at the hospital.' There was a momentary silence and Christy heard Adam sigh. 'I'd like to be charitable and say it's an urgent case that's keeping him from his packed waiting-room, but I suspect it has something to do with his wife and his new son, and I also suspect that the something is not strictly medical.'

'I'm sorry to disturb you, then.'

'That's OK, Christy,' Adam said, recovering his placid tone. 'Having trouble reading another script?'

'No.' Christy swiftly outlined her concerns with Mrs Haddon. 'I should phone the police, Adam. Yet I don't want to.'

'I don't blame you.' To Christy's relief Adam

sounded as hesitant as she was. 'Tell you what, Christy. I'll have Bella look up the lady's file here and ring you back.'

'I'd be grateful.'

Christy put down the phone, aware of an almost irrational gratitude for Adam's concern. Her worry about Mrs Haddon lifted slightly, and it was only because he had made her feel that the worry was shared.

Ten minutes later she lifted the phone to Adam again. He sounded as though he was frowning.

'There's not a lot here, Christy. Amy Haddon's seen Kate twice over the last two years. She's never been prescribed benzodiazepenes by Kate, but looking back there was a history with old Doc Macguire. He gave her tranquillisers after her husband died, but that's going back six years.'

Christy was silent for a moment. 'So she's Kate's patient,' she said. 'She's never seen Richard?'

'No.'

Again silence.

'I can't leave this until Kate's well enough to see her, can I?'

'No, you can't, Christy.' Adam said gently. 'Not if she's using stolen scripts.'

'Do I have to go to the police?'

Adam considered. 'I think the police have to know,' he said finally. 'But Christy, it would be much better for Mrs Haddon if she were the one to tell them.'

'I guess so.'

'Would you like me to go and see her?'

Yes, Christy thought. That was just what she would like. She'd like to shove the whole sticky problem aside, and if Adam was willing to take responsibility. . .

'No,' she said reluctantly. 'I know Amy Haddon, and she trusts me. If Kate can't go then I'm the logical choice.'

'When will you do it?' Adam said, and by his tone Christy knew he was forcing her to come to a decision.

'I'll go after work tonight. She. . .she only lives a block from here.'

'You'll be able to hobble?'

'Yes.'

'Is it seventeen Church Street?' Adam was reading the address from the card.

'Yes.'

'I'll collect you from there at six-thirty,' he told her.

'I can catch a taxi.'

'I know,' Adam said firmly. 'I'll be there at six-thirty.'

CHAPTER SIX

THE day dragged. Christy's visit to Mrs Haddon hung over her like a lead weight. Finally at five-thirty she locked the shop with more reluctance than she'd ever felt.

It was an easy stroll to Mrs Haddon's, which was just as well considering Christy's ineptitude on crutches. It took her longer than she thought, mostly because of the constant enquiries she had from the locals. Christy had a bandaged foot and a new nephew. The combination made everyone stop and talk.

Finally she made it. The house had a neat brick veneer, and was set behind rows of carefully ordered marigolds, petunias and zinnias. The ordered neatness looked out of place against the backdrop of towering gums in the bushland behind the town.

Mrs Haddon answered the door on the first ring. Her smile of welcome died as she saw Christy. Seconds later it was back in place as she recovered, but Christy hadn't been able to miss the look of dismay on the woman's face.

'Christy, love. How nice. Come on in. I'm. . . I'm just in the middle of cooking my chop for tea.'

Christy followed her through the hall into the kitchen beyond. She seated herself at the kitchen table while Amy turned down the heat under the frying-pan and put the kettle on to boil.

'Because you will have a cup of tea, won't you, dear?' Amy smiled nervously. 'Though I guess I should be offering you champagne, what with all the excitement of yesterday. A new little nephew. . .'

'Mrs Haddon, do you know why I'm here?' Christy broke in.

Amy's broad face stilled. She put a hand up, as if warding off what was coming, and then lowered herself on to a chair on the opposite side of the table to Christy.

'Is it. . .is it about my prescription?'

'Yes.'

'I. . . I really did lose the packet. . .'

Christy shook her head. 'It doesn't matter. That's not why I'm here. Mrs Haddon, your script was written on a stolen prescription form.'

There was a deathly silence. Amy stared across at Christy, her eyes blank and trapped. Christy met her look. She said nothing.

The silence dragged on and on. The kitchen clock sounded like the ticking of a bomb in the stillness. And then Amy Haddon's head dropped to her hands on the table and she wept.

Christy let her cry. It was no use supporting her yet, mouthing platitudes of comfort when she didn't know what was going on. It was for Amy to tell her. And finally Amy did, brokenly, between sobs, while, unnoticed her dinner turned to charcoal in the frying-pan behind them.

Christy listened. There was nothing she could do to alleviate the woman's distress. At some time during the sad little story she reached forward and took Amy's hand, but she didn't ask questions. She didn't need to.

It dated from Bill Haddon's death. Maybe before that, Amy thought. They had a son, but Tom and his father had fought and Amy hadn't seen him for eight years. She'd pretended to people in the town that he was working overseas — that he'd met a nice girl in America and settled down. It was all lies. Then, when Bill had died, there was nothing.

So one day she'd gone to Dr Macguire. She'd broken down and cried and told him how lonely she was, and how depressed. She'd confessed she had thought of suicide. Doc Macguire had been busy and not really

interested but he'd given her Valium. It hadn't solved
the problem — just pushed it back a bit, and then, after
a while, the Valium didn't work so well and she needed
more.

'You'd never asked Kate for a script?' Christy
probed.

'You get to know the doctors who'll give it to you,
no questions asked,' Amy said sadly. 'And I knew. . .
The first time I went to Kate I knew she wouldn't, at
least, not in the quantities I needed. And Dr Blair was
the same.' She sighed. 'I usually don't have my scripts
filled here either, only my car's playing up and I'm not
game to drive it so far.'

Christy nodded. 'And Dr Cartwright's scripts?' she
said gently.

The woman looked up, her face blotched and swollen
from weeping. 'I didn't know they were stolen, Christy.
Honest I didn't.'

'Dr Cartwright didn't write the script, though, did
he?' Christy insisted.

No.' Amy took a deep breath, stood up and crossed
to a kitchen drawer. A prescription pad lay just inside.

'I knew it was wrong.' Amy handed the pad over to
Christy. 'But. . .but it was getting so hard. The doctors
were getting more and more rude. The one I went to
all the time in Melbourne had trouble with the medical
board and stopped seeing patients — so I had to keep
going to new doctors and then the chemist in Tynong
said he wasn't filling any more scripts for tranquillisers.
I was so upset. It was hard enough going to Melbourne
for scripts, as well as getting them filled there. And
then. . .' She took a deep breath. 'There was a young
man in the Tynong chemist shop when they made all
that fuss. He followed me out, and offered to sell me
the pad.'

'The prescription pad?'

'Yes.' She sank to her chair again and looked wildly
up at Christy. 'I knew I shouldn't. But then, I thought

I wouldn't have to make the trip to Melbourne to doctors all the time. I knew what the prescription was supposed to say. And it worked. The first time I brought one in to you it worked.'

Christy nodded. It had. There was hardly a sure-fire way of protecting herself against fraud such as this. It would involve her telephoning every doctor who wrote a script.

'What. . .what are you going to do?' Amy asked fearfully and Christy shook her head.

'Mrs Haddon,' she said gently. 'The question's not what am I going to do, it's what are *you* going to do.'

'You mean. . .you mean you won't go to the police?'

Christy sighed. 'The pads were stolen, Mrs Haddon.'

'I know.' She nodded. 'At least. . .at least I suppose I should have known. I just blocked it out. . .'

There was the sound of a car pulling up outside. Amy's head jerked up. 'You. . .' her face was paper-white '. . .you've reported me.'

'It's not the police,' Christy reassured her. 'It's Dr McCormack.'

'Why. . .?'

'He's come to collect me,' Christy told her. 'But Mrs Haddon, you need help. You're in trouble. The trouble with the police is a minor issue. You're addicted to benzodiazepenes and you need a good doctor. Why not speak to Adam now?'

Amy shook her head. 'I couldn't,' she said helplessly.

'You're taking more Valium every day,' Christy said gently. 'Aren't you?'

'Y-yes.'

'Could you stop taking them—just like that? Could you give me the tablets now and never take one again?'

Amy was crying hard now into her hands. 'I couldn't,' she sobbed. 'I've tried. Oh, Christy. . . I honestly think I'd go mad.'

Christy took her hands firmly between her own. 'Then let us help you,' she said gently. 'That's Dr

McCormack's job. He knows how to help you. You're in trouble, Amy. No one's going to throw you in gaol, but you're moving outside the law now and there's nothing down that road but heartache and ruin. So let us help.'

A knock at the front door announced Adam's presence. Christy said nothing. The knocking sounded again.

Amy looked up, wiping a hand fiercely across her cheek. 'He. . .he really can help me?'

'You're not the first person this has happened to,' Christy assured her. 'There's a whole organisation — TRANX — specifically set up to help. Adam — Dr McCormack — is your starting point. Can I let him in?'

Mrs Haddon took a deep breath and rose. She visibly fought for and found control. 'I'll let him in,' she said, with quiet dignity, and Christy let her breath out in a sigh of relief.

'Would you like me to stay?'

The woman shook her head, her face resolute. 'No, thank you, Christy. I can do this. . .'

Christy nodded gravely, collected her crutches and followed Amy into the hall. The front door was open by the time she got there, and Adam was standing on the front porch.

'Christy says you might. . .you might be willing to help me,' Mrs Haddon was saying.

Adam looked down at the tear-stained lady before him, his green eyes gentle and understanding.

'It's my job, Mrs Haddon,' he said softly, unknowingly reiterating Christy's assurance. 'I understand you're Kate's patient, but if you'd like me to help. . .'

'Yes, please,' she said.

He took her arm and drew her inside.

Adam had left the car unlocked. Christy went out and sat in the passenger seat, content to leave them be.

She'd seen enough to be satisifed that indeed Adam

could help. Christy thought back to the expression in
Adam's eyes as he had promised assistance. No wonder
the man was an obstetrician, she thought. A frightened
mother enduring a difficult birth would be reassured by
Adam McCormack. He exuded competence, calm and
kindness.

Why on earth had he abandoned his obstetric practice to come here? Christy wondered for the hundredth
time. It didn't make any sense. He'd obviously left
people behind that he cared for. She shook her head.
The man was an enigma. He made no sense at all.

Finally he joined her. Mrs Haddon stood on the
front porch and waved them off, her smile a trifle
tremulous, but a smile none the less.

'Is it. . .will she be all right?' Christy asked softly as
they rounded the bend and were out of sight of the
house.

'She'll be OK tonight,' Adam said, frowning. 'It's
going to be a long haul, though.'

'And the police?'

'She and I are going to visit the police tomorrow.'
He glanced down at her. 'I'll ring them first and tell
them what's going on, just to make sure I don't get
some officious young constable throwing the book at
her, but Mrs Haddon will think she's confessing all.'

Christy nodded. 'She needs to do that.' She hesitated. 'Do you think they'll charge her?'

'I can't imagine that they will. It's a first offence, and
she's confessing. They might be interested in the chap
she bought the pads from, though. Very interested.'

'So she'll be OK?'

Adam frowned as he manoeuvred the little car round
a tight bend. 'Solving her addiction is not solving her
problem,' he said bluntly. 'She seems totally isolated,
cutting herself off from the community because she
thinks everyone feels sorry for her and she fears
questions about her son. Do you know anything
about him?'

'I don't.'

'She hasn't seen him since before her husband died.' Adam tapped his fingers on the steering-wheel. 'If the son left because he didn't get on with dad, maybe someone should let him know his dad's dead.'

'Mrs Haddon doesn't know where he is.'

'There are organisations that could help.'

'She'd be too proud to ask.'

'But I wouldn't.' Adam glanced down at her. 'Would our receptionist be able to give me his particulars?'

Christy grinned. 'Bella could tell you how many times every resident in this town has sneezed during their lifetime. She'd know everything there was to know.'

'And she can be trusted to keep things to herself.'

'Of course.'

Adam's face cleared. 'OK. We'll get the sleuth-hounds into action tomorrow. It's a long shot that we'll find him, but if we did and he could be persuaded to visit it might make a difference.'

'It certainly could.'

Adam looked down at her and smiled. 'Nice work, Christy.'

'Me?' She shook her head. 'I didn't do anything.'

'There are a lot of pharmacists in this world who'd ring the police and shrug the whole thing off as none of their business. There's a heart under that grumpy exterior.' And then, at the look on her face, he laughed. 'Come on, Christy, girl. We have a dinner date.'

'A dinner date?'

'Corrook's pub waits. I can hear a steak calling from here.'

The pub was quiet. Tuesday night was never busy. Most of the district saved their night out for market day or the weekend. The waitress brought them a drink, beamed once at Christy, half a dozen times at Adam, and left them to it.

'You're livening up Corrook no end,' Christy observed blandly, watching the waitress's obvious coquetry and thinking back to Ruth's reaction.

'How so?' Adam took a mouthful of beer and sat back, contented to watch the girl before him.

'No wife,' Christy told him. 'You're perceived as eligible.'

'I doubt I'm very eligible.'

'Why not?' Having gone this far Christy suddenly couldn't stop.

Adam's face clouded and Christy bit her lip. What on earth had made her say that? His wife had only been dead for six months after all, and if he loved her then the pain would still be raw. 'Oh, Adam, I'm sorry,' she said urgently, horrified at herself, and then, as the look on his face didn't clear, she reached forward and laid her hand on his. 'That was stupid and insensitive of me. I'm sorry.'

He shrugged but the pain behind his eyes stayed. 'I guess it's true,' he said harshly. 'I'm footloose and fancy-free.' He looked up and met her eyes. 'And, as you say, eligible.'

Was it longing for the dead Sarah that was causing the pain behind his eyes? Or was there some woman back in England he was in love with? Some love-affair he was escaping by coming here? She thought back to the middle-of-the-night phone call. Maybe the pain was because he missed her — what was the name he had asked for? Fiona. . . It was suddenly important that the pain was for his wife.

'Why did you come?' she asked gently. She touched his hand again. 'Am I wrong in thinking you've left more than an obstetric practice in England?'

His eyes widened, startled. Christy met his look. There was a long silence. The waitress came around and took their order, beamed again at Adam, came back and offered them another drink, beamed at Adam again and finally left them alone.

'I shouldn't have asked that,' Christy said softly. 'It's none of my business.'

Adam shook his head. 'I'd like to tell you,' he said. 'But I can't, Christy.' His voice broke suddenly and the hand under hers turned itself into a clenched fist. 'I can't. It's too damned raw. . . I——' He broke off. 'Did I just order dinner? What the hell did I order?'

'T-bone steak,' Christy smiled, withdrawing her hand.

'And chips?'

'There's no choice about the chips.'

Oh.' He grinned then, the pain in his eyes receding, and Christy was aware that he was making almost a superhuman effort. 'That's all right, then. I'm sorry. I guess I'm just homesick.'

'After three days,' she teased him, striving for lightness. 'You should have packed your teddy bear.'

The pain surfaced again, a flash of raw agony, so real that Christy flinched. What on earth was driving the man?

'As you say,' he said blankly.

They made small talk through the rest of their dinner, both aware of the strained atmosphere. It was all Christy could do to eat. She'd hurt Adam. Regardless of what was driving him — what his reasons for being here were — she'd hurt him and she would just as willingly have kicked her broken toe.

Mandy helped. Their waitress for the night was making a flagrant play for the new doctor. She'd eyed the couple since they'd come in, noted Christy's hand meeting Adam's over the table, and then, with unerring intuition, sense their withdrawal from each other. With barracuda subtlety she moved in for the kill.

'It's so nice to see you out and about,' she purred to Adam. 'I know you're boarding with Miss Blair here, but it can get so dull staying home every night. You're always welcome here, you know. I work Monday to Saturday.' She gave her hips a slight wiggle. 'And

Sunday is my day off. Not that I can't get another night off if there's an invitation too good to miss.' She sighed. 'There's no man in this town worth missing work over, though. At least, not till now.'

Christy choked on her lemon squash and Adam assumed a suitably sympathetic expression.

'I'll be in the surgery tomorrow to see you,' Mandy promised, encouraged. She carefully ignored Christy's undignified coughing fit. 'I've the most appalling bunions, Doctor. The Melbourne specialist told me he'd never seen bunions like them. Wanted to cut them off, he did, but I would have been on crutches for weeks. No, thanks, I said. There's something really unattractive about a woman on crutches, don't you think, Miss Blair?'

'Absolutely,' Christy agreed weakly.

'Anyway, I'm sure all they need is a nice sympathetic doctor who knows what they're all about,' Mandy continued. 'And as soon as I saw you I said to myself, There's a doctor I wouldn't mind showing my bunions to.'

'That's. . .that's very nice of you, Miss. . .?' Adam managed.

'Mandy,' their waitress told him expansively. 'If you're going to see my bunions, then we should be on first-name terms.'

'I couldn't agree more,' Adam told her, straight-faced. 'What do you call your bunions?'

Mandy flashed him a look as though suspecting him of laughing at her, but Adam's expression was dead-pan. She giggled forgivingly.

'Oh, you are a one, Doctor.' The cook was gesticulating angrily from the kitchen and she waved him down. 'I have to go,' she apologised. 'Joe's so impatient. It won't hurt table four to wait for their dinner.' She beamed again. 'I'll see you tomorrow, then.'

'I'll look forward to it,' Adam promised. Mandy

tottered away on her stilettos and Christy emerged from her handkerchief.

'Wow,' she breathed. 'I've been living in Corrook for two years and I've never seen Mandy's bunions.'

'Have you wanted to?' Adam asked, startled.

'Mandy's bunions have been a topic of conversation in the Corrook pub ever since I've been here,' Christy told him. 'Richard was allowed a peek once, and swears they do exist, but until now. . .' She reached for her crutches and stood. 'If you've seen Mandy's bunions, then you've arrived at the height of Corrook society.'

'Better than the corgis?'

'Much better.'

Adam nodded. 'And to think I once believed Corrook was socially behind London.' He smiled down at her. 'You don't want to stay for coffee?'

'No fear,' Christy said firmly. 'Mandy's getting so excited she might expose them on the spot.'

They drove home in silence, both deep in their own thoughts. Christy was aware that she was bone-weary. The last few nights of not enough sleep were catching up with her and her foot was aching in sympathy with her tired body.

Adam pulled up in front of the house and came round to open the door for her.

'How's your foot?' he asked, handing her the crutches.

'Fine.'

He shook his head in the moonlight. 'You make a lousy liar, Christy Blair.' Without further comment he stooped and lifted her into his arms. 'Let's give it a rest, shall we?'

Christy gave an undignified yelp of astonishment. 'Put me down, Adam!'

'Sure.' In a few easy strides he had her on to the veranda and was lowering her on to the cane lounger. 'Your wish is my command, my Christy. Now stay here while I make coffee.'

'But I don't want coffee.'

He sighed. 'Are you just being difficult, Christy Blair?'

She was still feeling breathless from the feel of his arms around her. She looked up at his stern features. He stood, his arms crossed, daring her to keep being starchy. She couldn't.

'I'm just being difficult,' she agreed in a small voice, and then subsided into silence while Adam went inside and made coffee.

The night was hot and still. They left the veranda light off to discourage the bugs, and drank their coffee by moonlight. Christy was drifting in a haze of unreality. Adam gave her a couple of pain-killers with her coffee and as they took effect she felt almost light-headed.

They didn't speak. It was almost as if each was afraid to. Every time I open my mouth I say the wrong thing, Christy thought bitterly, so therefore I won't open my mouth.

Adam must be feeling the same. He was content to let the cicadas in the bush around them do the talking, and Christy's beloved nightjars.

Finally she rose uncertainly. The night, the warmth and the silence were doing strange things to her. It wasn't anything to do with Adam, she told herself. It was the pain-killers.

'I'm going to bed,' she said uncertainly.

He rose and came towards her, and Christy saw what he intended. 'No.' She warded him off with her hands. 'I can walk.'

'Being scratchy again?'

She shook her head. He was so close. . . 'No,' she said again weakly. 'Not. . .not scratchy.'

He stood looking down at her in the moonlight, her fair curls reflecting the faint light back up at him. She didn't look up. She didn't move. Having said she was going, it seemed now it was almost impossible that she should.

His hand came to her chin, forcing her face up so that he could see her expression. As she looked up she saw her own confusion reflected in Adam's dark eyes.

It was the night, she told herself savagely. It was the moon and the silence and the heavy scent of the gums all around. It was almost intoxicating. Leading them to madness. . .

Adam bent his head and kissed her.

For a moment she held herself stiff and unyielding. This was what she had most feared. This. . .the feel of this man holding her as he had held her five years ago. He had kissed her then and she had tumbled head over heels in love with him — a stupid teenage love for a married man.

And she was still in love with him. His kiss was what she wanted above all else. His hands came up and gripped the smooth skin of her arms. His lips were light and questioning, not demanding. She fought. . . she fought to hold herself back but she was lost and she knew it. She had been lost for five years. Her lips parted gently under his and she returned his kiss.

The night blurred into a haze of love and desire. The moonlight ceased to be. Christy could no longer hear the cicadas, or the eerie call of the nightjars close by. She had senses for nothing but Adam.

It didn't make sense. He had made no attempt to talk to her — to tell her he wanted her. All he was doing was kissing a girl because the night was lovely, he was lonely and Christy was close. She knew it. This after all was what had happened before, but, like before, she could not resist. Not while Adam wanted her. Her lips parted to deepen the kiss. Her hands came up to hold his hard male body against her. She wanted him so much. . . It didn't matter for how long. For just this moment, if that was all there was.

The harsh jangle of the telephone cut into the night.

For a moment they ignored it, and then slowly, reluctantly, the man and woman drew apart.

Christy backed off, a step back from Adam, reality rushing back in. It was as if the telephone was an alarm. Her eyes were wide and fearful. The magic was broken and the fears flooded back. She had made vows to treat this man as a friend. She had vowed not to expose herself and what had she done? Her breath drew in on a jagged sob.

'Christy. . .' Adam said, and his voice was a mixture of tenderness and uncertainty. 'Christy, love. . .'

'You. . .you'd better answer the phone,' she said bleakly.

He had no choice. The phone's shrill ring still cut across the stillness. It demanded an answer. With one final uncertain glance at Christy, Adam turned to go inside.

Christy stayed exactly where she was. She couldn't have moved if she'd wanted to. It was as if her world had stopped turning—freezing her in an endless limbo. She wanted Adam so much that it was a physical ache and he was striding into the house away from her.

As she heard him talk urgently into the phone she shuddered once and then was still again. She felt deathly cold.

'A child with an angry appendix,' Adam said as he returned. 'Richard's scrubbing now. Christy. . .'

'You have to go,' she said dully. 'I know.'

'Christy. . .' He took her arm and the feel of his hand on her bare skin made her recoil as if touching something that could bite or sting.

'Don't touch me,' she whispered.

'Why. . .?' His face creased into a frown. 'Christy, I though you wanted me to. . .'

'You thought I wanted you to kiss me? Well, I don't, Adam McCormack. I let you kiss me and I was crazy. Crazy, do you hear? I don't want you to kiss me. I don't want you to touch me, ever again.'

'You wanted me to kiss you as much as I wanted to kiss you.' Adam's voice was flat and emotionless — imparting a fact. It stopped Christy's mounting hysteria in its tracks.

'Yes,' she said dully when she had regained her breath. She didn't look at him. 'I did. I was stupid. Let's just say we were both of us carried away with the moment, then. The night and the wine. . .'

'You drank lemon squash and I had two low-alcohol beers.'

'You have to go,' she told him harshly. 'Remember?'

'I have to go,' he agreed. 'I remember.' He touched her lightly on the cheek, ignoring her instinctive protest. 'Contrary to what you believe, Christy Blair, I have a very good memory.'

CHAPTER SEVEN

THE next couple of weeks were the most difficult Christy had ever known. She slept badly. She worked harder than she had ever done and she lost weight.

'What on earth is going on, Christy?' Kate demanded when Christy dropped in after work one night. Kate and the baby were out on the veranda, mid-feed. In contrast to Christy, Kate was blooming.

'What do you mean?'

'I mean you look like death,' Christy's sister-in-law told her frankly. 'Richard and I are worried about you.'

'Nice of you,' Christy said drily, and then winced at Kate's look. 'I'm sorry, Kate. I know you are. I'm. . . It's just that I'm working too hard.'

'Why?'

'I'm covering scripts for an extra,' she said defensively.

'When I was working full-time you were as busy as you are now. It didn't seem to get you down then.'

Christy shook her head bleakly. 'Maybe it's just my boarder, then,' she said. 'It. . .it makes me tense having him in the house all the time.'

'You're not sleeping?' Kate probed.

'Not. . .not very well.'

'Hmm.' Kate shifted the baby from one breast to the other, placing a kiss on his downy head in the process. 'Now if I were Doc Macguire I'd prescribe Valium. Instead. . .instead I'll ask you what's wrong.'

Christy shook her head again bleakly, but Kate was not so easily silenced.

'Christy, whatever the problem is, it's not going to go away of its own accord, is it?' she probed.

'No.' She knew that was true. Adam seemed to be

84

settling down to stay at least for a few months. He'd
built himself a routine which incorporated Christy's
house as his home and apart from kicking him out to
the pub or to stay with Kate and Richard there seemed
no escape.

Since the night they had kissed she had abandoned
any intention of treating him as a friend. She treated
him now with bare civility and nothing more.

And Adam. . . Adam was busy, and their times at
home together were few. The morning after he had
kissed her he had tried to talk to her, but Christy would
have none of it.

'If you touch me again, Adam McCormack, I'll
scream so loudly the police at Tynong will hear.'

To her surprise Adam had looked at her in silence,
then nodded and accepted her ultimatum without argument. It was as if he too was having second thoughts
and he welcomed her coldness. Their brief time of
friendship — of intimacy — was over.

Which would be OK if only he'd pack his bags and
leave, Christy thought desperately. But he wouldn't.
He filled the house with the smell of him, his size and
his tired green eyes which looked almost as strained as
her own.

They were strained. The kiss must have been a result
of that strain, Christy decided, not because he had
really wanted to kiss her. Things seemed to be going
wrong for Dr McCormack as well as for herself. Often
she heard him rise in the night and make a phone call
and it didn't take much imagination to know it was
England he called. Over and over again she put her
pillow over her head in dismay, blocking the sound of
his voice. Damn him. Damn him for ever coming back
into her life.

All this must have been shadowing her face. Christy
came back to the present to find Kate's thoughtful eyes
on her.

'It is Adam, isn't it?' Kate said gently.

Christy flushed and stood up. 'I have to go,' she said. 'I. . . I have shelves I want to clear tonight.'

'To stop you going home to Adam?'

'No.'

'Christy. . .'

Christy stood, her hands on her slim hips, looking defiantly down at this girl she called her friend. Kate was her friend, she knew, and by marrying her brother Kate was also her family. If there was one thing Christy needed now it was family — a shoulder to weep on — and Kate was the nearest thing offering.'Yes.' Her resolve suddenly faded and she sat down heavily on the step. She was going crazy. Kate couldn't help but at least she would listen. 'Yes, Kate.' Her voice broke on a sob. 'To stop me going home to Adam.'

'You're in love with him?' Kate asked gently.

'Yes.'

Silence. Then Kate sighed. 'How long have you been in love with him, Christy?'

'For five years.'

Even if she had been able to make her voice sound as it should, the story must seem stupid, she thought bitterly, a student falling head over heels in love with her brother's friend and staying in love for this long. Adam had made no promises. He had broken no trust, but Christy was breaking her heart. Somehow she managed to tell Kate, though, and if it sounded stupid then at least in the telling the awful isolation she was feeling eased.

When she finally finished — when her voice had trailed off to a hiccuping sob at the end — she half expected Kate to laugh. Instead Kate laid the sleeping baby into his pram and came down to sit beside Christy on the step. There was silence for a long time.

'Christy, I think Richard might have made a mistake,' Kate said at last.

'In asking Adam to come here?' Christy gave a humourless laugh. 'Of course he didn't. Corrook needs

Dr Adam McCormack. Even I can see that. It's me who doesn't.'

Kate shook her head. 'I didn't mean that. I meant in not telling you about Adam's background.'

Christy stiffened and stared at her sister-in-law. 'You mean you know?'

Kate shrugged. 'Christy, Richard still thinks of you as his little sister. Rightly or wrongly, there are things he'll tell me that he thinks are unsuitable for his little sister to hear.'

'Even though I'm twenty-six.'

Kate smiled. 'To Richard, you're still twelve.'

'Such as?' Christy demanded.

Kate sighed. 'It's not my story to tell, but I do think. . . Christy, did you only meet Sarah the once?'

'Adam's wife?'

'Yes.'

Christy nodded.

'You never knew what was wrong with her?'

'The reason she died, you mean? I asked Adam and he wouldn't tell me.'

'I don't know the reason she died, although I can guess,' Kate said sadly. 'But Sarah had been ill for a very long time before she died. She was schizophrenic.'

'Schizophrenic. . .' Christy stared at Kate as if she had taken leave of her senses. She shook her head. 'I met her, Kate. She was sane. . .'

'What do you know about schizophrenia?'

Christy shook her head. 'Only the drugs and their dosages,' she admitted. 'The treatment's a pretty savage regime.'

'It is at that,' Kate said sadly. 'It has to be.' She hesitated as though considering what to say and then shrugged. She'd gone this far and she knew she couldn't retreat. Christy had to know.

'Sarah was a lawyer,' Kate said slowly. 'According to Richard she was beautiful and brilliant, vivacious and funny.' She gave a rueful smile. 'The sort of lady you don't like to hear your husband describing. Anyway, Adam met her and married her. Six months later things started to go dreadfully wrong.'

'The schizophrenia surfaced?'

'Yes.' Kate bit her lip. 'According to Richard, it was sudden and appalling. Sarah decided Adam wanted her dead. She told everyone who would listen, and at first she sounded sane. She even had Adam arrested. Adam went through hell, trying to get other people to believe there was something medically wrong, and trying to persuade Sarah to accept treatment. Adam lost a good many friends before Sarah's behaviour grew so bizarre she was no longer credible.'

'So what happened?'

'She broke down completely one night. Rang the police and said Adam was chasing her with knives, but then threw in a few demons for good effect. By the time the police arrived she was convinced it was any male trying to kill her. She attacked a policeman with kitchen scissors and ended arrested herself.'

'Oh, God,' Christy murmured. 'Oh, Adam. . .'

'She was treated then,' Kate said, 'but the treatment never restored Sarah as Adam had first known her. She continued with periods of thinking Adam was persecuting her. She abandoned the legal profession and went modelling, swinging on highs and lows like a manic depressive. Adam seemed to have no place in her life. I gather she filed for divorce. That was the stage they'd reached when Richard took Adam to your home for the week.'

Kate's voice trailed off, letting her words sink home. Christy needed the silence — she stared sightlessly ahead, appalled.

So this had been the tragedy Richard had mentioned — the reason Adam had needed a break from the hospital. His wife had abandoned him to her madness. So Adam had come. He had met Christy, a normal, cheerful student full of life and laughter. Who could blame Adam for finding respite in her company? Christy put a hand up to wipe away angry tears. Why hadn't Richard told her this? Why hadn't he? She would have been so much. . .

She stopped mid-thought and knew why Richard hadn't told her. She would have treated Adam with sympathy and maybe the last thing he'd needed then was sympathy.

'Only I gather Sarah appeared halfway through Adam's break,' Kate continued. 'She'd just changed medication and it was working, and she'd suddenly remembered she had a husband. So Adam went. . .'

Christy nodded. Of course he would.

'I don't know much more about the next few years,' Kate told her. 'Neither does Richard. After that break Adam cut himself off from most of his friends. Richard gathered that Sarah swung from frantic highs to low bouts of depression and paranoia. She hated the side-effects of the drugs so whenever she started feeling good she'd abandon the medication. Richard assumes she either suicided in a bout of depression or had an accident in one of her manic phases. He doesn't ask.'

Christy said nothing. She couldn't. She was feeling ill.

'Christy?'

She looked up then to find Kate staring at her with worried eyes. She managed a smile. 'So in the middle of all this Dr McCormack takes out his friend's sister and kisses her goodnight,' she said bitterly. 'Then she tumbles head over heels in love with him and can't understand why he doesn't even notice.' She stood up abruptly. 'Thank you for telling me, Kate. I wish I'd known. . .'

'Would it have made a difference?'

'To me loving him?' Christy shook her head. 'I don't suppose it would, really. But maybe I can stop blaming Adam and cope with my feelings without hurting him further.'

She left Kate sitting on the veranda, and drove her little car down towards the town. She wasn't going home yet. She didn't want to face Adam until she'd had time to absorb the things she'd learned.

It was almost dusk. The last faint tinges of crimson were fading from the sky, above the canopy the gums made over the road. Christy glanced at her watch. Seven p.m. She'd sort shelves at the pharmacy for an hour.

She swung her car into the street leading to the main road and slowed. This was the road Mrs Haddon lived on. A rusty orange car was parked out the front and Mrs Haddon's front door was wide open.

Christy was preoccupied and distressed but suddenly that preoccupation was pierced. Something was wrong. Or was it?

There could be a thousand logical reasons for Mrs Haddon's open door but Christy slowed still further. She was remembering the woman's careful greeting of both herself and Adam. As each had arrived she had greeted them, closed the door behind them and hooked the chain firmly in place. To Christy it had almost seemed like being locked in, and later, when she had left and Adam had stayed, it had seemed downright obsessive as Mrs Haddon had carefully locked Adam in and Christy out. Christy had called in several times over the last two weeks and each time she had been welcomed in and the door carefully closed behind her.

So why was the door open?

It's a hot night, Christy told herself. Maybe she's trying to get some air through the place.

But it's been hot for the last two weeks. . .an inner voice argued.

She pulled to a halt behind the rusty car. It was old and looked unroadworthy. Its rear was plastered with distinctly unsavoury stickers. Christy hadn't seen it before and that too made her nervous. She knew the local ones.

'Maybe it's her son. Maybe.' She was talking aloud in an effort to make herself believe but her voice sounded unconvinced.

Reluctantly she climbed from the car. She hoped desperately that it was Amy's son, but she wasn't convinced enough to drive on. She might be interrupting but she could always just say a brief hello and depart again. She walked up the front path on to the porch — and stopped dead. A low moan came through the door to meet her, and then a voice raised in sadistic malice.

'You thought I couldn't guess who dobbed me in? You have to be kdiding. Two hundred lousy bucks you gave me for that pad and it's not worth the slammer for two hundred bucks. If I'm going to go, then I'll make it worthwhile.' There was a sickening thud, a whimper of pure terror, a crash and then silence.

Christy should have gone for help. She should have run, but even as she thought it the whimper of terrified pain knifed through her and she moved. She launched herself through the passage to the living-room like a wild cat, shock and fury driving her on. She went straight for the lout standing over the woman on the floor.

Like a feral cat attacking something much bigger, she fought. Until that moment Christy would have described herself as a coward, but there was nothing of the coward about her now. She clung and kicked and scratched and fought, clinging with a ferocity that left the dim-witted lout nowhere to go.

He was stronger than she. The fight could only go one way, but Christy had the advantage of surprise. He hit her once, hard, knocking the wind out of her as he sent her sprawling across the room, and gave a grunt of satisfaction at what he had done. He didn't expect what happened. Christy didn't draw breath. She bounced back as if the smashing blow had hardly struck and was back into the fray, her semi-healed foot kicking for all it was worth, making him swear with pain and lunge again.

This time her tactics were different. She ducked her head and butted him straight in the solar plexus, her knee coming up to deliver the cruellest blow she could think of. He yelped in pain, and then grabbed her hair, drawing her hard up against him. Christy screamed for all she was worth and stomped down square on his bare feet. It was a mistake. In blind fury he smashed into her face again. Christy slumped to the floor as his grip slackened and the blow took effect. She put her hands up in a futile gesture to ward off another blow but it didn't come.

She had help. She had Adam.

He had made no sound, appearing from nowhere. As the lout's hand came up to smash into Christy, Adam caught it from behind. From that moment what happened seemed almost in slow motion. Christy stared up through a pain-shrouded mist to see Adam turn her attacker around. It seemed as if he positioned him, took careful aim and then slammed him harder than Christy knew anyone could hit. The lout was flung against the far wall, but almost before he struck the wall Adam was there, following through, twisting him upright with his hand and pulling his arms up behind him. The lout was shoved blind into the corner of the room, his arms locked up behind him. Adam leaned against him, pushed his arms further until he was sure his opponent couldn't move an inch and then turned his head slightly.

'Christy?' His voice was hoarse with effort and concern.

She was dragging herself dazed from the floor. She staggered, raised her hand as if to clear her eyes and then managed to rise. 'Adam. . .' It was a tremulous whisper.

'Christy, can you call the police?'

She stared across at him as if she weren't seeing him,

then looked down at Mrs Haddon. The woman was unconscious on the floor, bleeding from a savage cut to her head.

'The police first,' Adam said urgently, his voice knifing through her haze. 'Christy, go. Dial 999.'

Christy cast one last glance at the unconscious woman at her feet and moved. Adam was right. The police first.

She dialled in a haze, from the phone in the kitchen, scarcely able to think of where she was and who she wanted. It was lucky the operator was trained to deal with shocked people. Finally Christy put the phone down, still not sure what she had said. The ambulance and the police were on their way, the operator had assured her. It didn't seem to matter much. She took another deep breath and made her unsteady way back to the sitting-room.

No one had moved. It was like some dramatic tableau on a video, where someone had pressed the pause button. Adam was still in his corner, the lout behind him locked in by his presence. He shifted slightly and then gave a savage grunt of pain as Adam's grip tightened.

'They're coming,' Christy said dully. She couldn't make her head work.

'Christy, you need to put some pressure on Amy's head,' Adam told her. And then, as she stared at him uncomprehendingly, she said it again. 'Christy! Are you OK?'

She took a deep breath.

'Come on, Christy,' Adam said, this time more gently. 'You can do it. She's bleeding and you have to stop it.'

The fog shifted slightly with his words. This was Adam here, and Adam needed her. The urge to let the blackness close in on her disappeared. She nodded, the faint movement hurting, but the blackness stayed back.

Amy Haddon had been bashed to unconsciousness.

Christy dropped to her knees, forcing herself to concentrate. The wound on Amy's scalp was oozing blood into the floral carpet. Adam had cause for concern. The wound was bleeding freely, the carpet disguising just how much blood there was.

A pad. Christy needed a pad. There would be something in the kitchen but she'd waste time. She was wearing a soft cotton blouse and skirt. Modesty could be put on hold for the time being. She ripped her blouse off, folded it fast into a firm pad and placed it against the wound.

'Good,' Adam approved, and then swore as his prisoner moved. 'You know,' he said idly as if talking to no one in particular, 'the bone in your arm is only designed to take a certain amount of pressure, and I'm applying that right now. If you move one fraction more you'll increase the pressure to breaking-point. And frankly, it would give me a great deal of satisfaction to break both your arms. Don't try me.' There was a moment's silence while his point went home, the lout in the corner subsided and then Adam turned his attention back to Christy. 'You need more pressure, Christy, love. The blood's coming through.'

'I'm trying.'

'Put the pressure at the base of the wound and on the actual laceration itself,' he told her. 'Double your pad. Make your pressure-point smaller.'

Christy nodded and did as she was told. Her head was clearing and the awful feeling of nausea was receding. She concentrated fiercely on the wound, trying to block out the white face of the lady on the floor. The blow to the head must have been savage to make her so deeply unconscious. What else had this creep done? Amy's arm was bent at a crazy angle. It must be broken. There was nothing Christy could do about that, though. There was only the bleeding that she had to stop.

And then the first siren came screaming from the

distance, followed by another. The dazed directions Christy had given must have been right. The sirens screamed closer and closer and then stopped dead. There was the sound of running feet and suddenly there were uniforms everywhere, and guns, and an ambulance officer was moving her gently aside to let Adam examine Amy. 'We'll take over now, miss. It's OK.'

She stood mute, unmoving, while Adam swiftly attended the injured woman. Christy didn't think. She didn't make a sound. The shaking of her body went on and on, until it seemed almost impossible to stand.

'That's a massive head injury,' Adam was saying grimly, as he set up a drip. 'There'll be internal bleeding.'

'Should we transfer her straight to Melbourne, Doc?' one of the ambulance officers asked. Adam shook his head.

'Let's get her to Theatre here first and see if we can stabilise the bleeding. Radio on ahead to the hospital. Tell Dr Blair he'll be needed, and tell Matron to prepare the theatre.'

He had done what he could for now. Finally Adam stood, handing control over to the ambulance officers. He looked across at the ashen-faced girl staring sightlessly down at Amy Haddon and then he had her in his arms and was holding her as if she was the most precious thing in the entire world. Christy sagged into his arms. She was safe and the blackness was allowed to take over.

She didn't faint. For a moment she thought she would. Her world spun in giddy whirls of relief and the warmth of Adam's arms and the strength of his shoulder under her head promised her safety. Now, when she could finally close her eyes, there was no longer the need. There was nothing to escape from. The lout was being hustled, handcuffed, out of the room. An ambulance officer was adjusting Mrs

Haddon's drip in readiness for transfer to a stretcher. Everything was under control and Christy was where she wanted to be. She stayed huddled into Adam's shoulder as he directed the ambulance officers and answered the policemen's brusque questions. She never wanted to move again.

It couldn't last. The moment of escape had to pass. As the stretcher holding Mrs Haddon left the room, the ambulance officer looked questioningly at Christy and Adam drew her away from him.

'Christy, love?' His voice was infinitely tender and it made her want to weep.

He saw her face closely then for the first time and what he saw made him swear with a ferocity Christy had never heard before.

'The bastard. Christy. . .' Adam shook his head in disbelief, his eyes black with anger. 'I should have broken his arms. I should have broken the bastard's neck.'

His shock made Christy give a tearful smile. She raised her fingers to her swelling face. 'Is it so bad?'

Adam closed his eyes and held her close again. She felt the anger in him, held forcibly in check. His hands were tight with fury.

'We'll take you down to the hospital,' the ambulance officer said firmly. 'Let's have her, Doc. Will you follow us down or will you come in the ambulance?'

'I'll bring Christy,' Adam said firmly.

'Adam, there's no need,' Christy interjected. Her voice shook as the effects of shock started to settle in. 'I. . . I can drive home.'

'Like hell you can,' Adam said savagely, and she started with the ferocity of his voice. He collected himself and gave a grim laugh. 'I'm sorry, Christy, love. I didn't mean to sound so. . .'

'Mrs Haddon will need you,' she told him. 'I don't need hospital.'

'You haven't looked in the mirror,' he told her.

'You've a cut above your ear that looks as if it needs a suture. I'm not letting you go until you've had a wash and we see what other damage is below that blood.'

Christy moved her hand to her ear. To her amazement her fingers came away sticky and wet. She stared down at the blood, bemused.

'I didn't feel that.'

'You'll feel it soon,' Adam promised. 'Now, are you coming or do I have to carry you?'

She smiled ruefully. 'Your *modus operandi* for reluctant women,' she teased him. A shudder suddenly caught her and she swayed. Adam's arm came around her and held her hard.

'Let's go, my Christy,' he told her.

He drove down to the hospital swiftly, glancing over at the girl beside him every few moments. His eyes were still black, his brow creased, and Christy had the impression that the swearing was still going on under his breath. The shuddering of her body was starting to ease as the warmth of the evening and the comfort of Adam's presence took hold. It seemed, though, that his anger was growing.

'It's OK,' she said tentatively to the man beside her. 'It's over. It's not as if he got away with it.'

'It's not over for Amy Haddon,' Adam said harshly. 'If that contusion is bleeding into the brain. . .' He swore out loud again and glanced across at her. 'I saw him hit you,' he said evenly. 'I heard you scream and got to the door just as he hit you. I thought he'd. . . I thought he'd killed you.'

'I was born tough,' Christy said unsteadily. 'It'd take more than a sneak thief to polish me off.'

'A murderer at the very least,' Adam agreed grimly. 'He damned near became one.' Then, as he dragged his attention back to the road, his hands clenched on the steering-wheel. 'He might yet be one.'

'She's not. . .she's not so badly hurt, is he?'

'I can't tell, Christy. We've no way of telling until we get her into Theatre.' He closed his eyes for a fraction of a second and when he opened them he seemed to have recovered. 'At least it's not you as well.'

At the hospital Christy was left in the charge of a nursing sister. Richard had arrived at the hospital, but Amy Haddon's injuries required both doctors.

'They're operating,' Sister Rowe told Christy, grim-faced, as she washed the blood from Christy's bruises.

'What for?'

The nurse shook her head. 'Mrs Haddon gained consciousness for a few minutes as she arrived at hospital, but she's lost consciousness again. That's all I know.'

'There's internal bleeding.' It was Kate, coming into the room behind them. 'Christy Blair, what on earth have you been up to?'

Christy stared at her sister-in-law in astonishment. Kate was still wearing the clothes Christy had seen her in an hour ago, but now she was also wearing her white medical coat.

'I'm back,' Kate said firmly. 'Don't look at me like that, Christy. Adam rang me to say you needed washing, stitching and TLC.'

'TLC. . .?'

'Tender loving care,' Kate said briskly. 'Item seven on the benefits schedule.'

'He. . .'

'They're operating fast on Amy,' Kate told her. 'When I finish here I'll go in and assist. There's internal haemorrhaging. Adam doesn't think she'd survive transfer to the city.'

'He's operating?'

'He and Richard.' Kate frowned. 'It's not something I'd like to tackle.'

'You should be there.' Christy grimaced as she thought what such an operation could mean. Three doctors would be much preferable to two.

'I will be,' Kate promised, her fingers touching the contusion over Christy's left ear with gentle skill. 'Just as soon as I've pulled you together.'

'The baby?'

'Andrew's in the nursery.' Kate lifted a syringe from the tray the nurse was holding and inspected it. 'I shouldn't admit this at the risk of sounding a bad mother,' she said, 'but I'm missing medicine like crazy. If I could get a really good baby-sitter I'd think about doing a few hours a week.' The syringe passed her inspection, and with practised ease she placed it against Christy's skin and drove it home. 'There. That's the worst you'll feel. Now, while I sew you up I want to hear the whole story, omitting nothing.'

Her handiwork over, Kate left Christy. 'Don't you drive home,' she said severely. 'Stay here and sleep off the shock.' She motioned to the nurse. 'See to it, Sister.'

'I'm needed in Theatre too,' the sister said diffidently. 'I'll tell the aide to check.'

Half an hour later Christy was climbing walls with impatience and worry. The hospital was deathly silent. Every available member of staff was in Theatre. The nursing aide came by periodically, no doubt under orders, tried to take Christy's temperature and offered her a cup of tea, but Christy rejected both. Finally she threw back the bedcovers and looked down ruefully at her bra and crushed skirt.

'I can hardly go home like this.'

To stay longer seemed equally impossible. She rose and walked out into the corridor.

The aide was in Sister's station. As Christy watched, a buzzer sounded and a light came on above the door of the ward next to hers. She drew back into her room and waited for the girl to pass. As she disappeared into the ward, Christy walked firmly down to Sister's station and picked up the phone.

'Pete's taxi, please,' she said firmly. Then, 'Can you

collect a passenger from outside the hospital immediately, please?'

She replaced the receiver and walked through into the staffroom. Here was what she was looking for. At the rear of the room were a row of pegs and one of her own white dispensing coats hung from one. She used it when she came into the hospital and prepared prescriptions in the small hospital dispensary. She pulled it on and then paused. There were footsteps coming down the corridor again. The nursing aide was returning.

She'd make a fuss. Christy knew as well as anyone that no aide would accept responsibility for discharging a patient. She'd insist on letting them know in Theatre and either Kate or Adam would try to dissuade her, distracting them unnecessarily from the task in hand.

There was an alternative. Christy crossed swiftly to the French windows overlooking the hospital garden and pulled them open. She reached the hospital drive just as Pete swung his taxi off the road. Five minutes later she was home.

CHAPTER EIGHT

CHRISTY phoned the hospital as soon as she arrived home. If the nursing aide found Christy gone, she would panic.

'When Adam. . .when the doctors finish in Theatre tell them I've gone,' Christy told the unfortunate aide. 'You're not to interrupt them before they've finished.'

'No, miss,' the girl said dubiously.

Christy put down the phone, satisfied that she was causing no trouble. Now she could head for where she most wanted to be. Her head ached unmercifully and her legs still felt like jelly. She walked into her bedroom and fell into bed.

Despite her exhaustion Christy couldn't sleep. Her head hurt. Her thoughts were still with the middle-aged lady fighting for her life in Theatre back at the hospital.

The anger that had stayed with her since she had walked through Amy's open door was slowly seeping out of her. It was replaced with bleak sorrow. How could such a thing happen to so kind-hearted a lady? Amy Haddon had lost a son and a husband. She'd stepped outside the law and now she'd almost paid for that with her life. And yet she was such an ordinary person. She didn't deserve what fate had dealt her. . .

As Adam hadn't deserved what fate had dealt him. The story Kate had told her earlier in the night came back to haunt her. She thought of Adam now, exhausted and fighting for the life of a woman he hardly knew. What drove him on? Why was he here? What demons was he escaping by coming to Australia?

She tossed in her bed, her foot aching and her head throbbing. At some stage she rose and found some pain-killers, then found herself staring at the two little white pills as though afraid to take them.

This is ridiculous she told herself. It's hardly habit-forming to take a couple of pain-killers after fighting to the death with a would-be murderer. She grinned reluctantly to herself at her dramatic description of the night's events, swallowed the pills and climbed back into bed. Still there was no sleep.

Finally she heard what she had been subconsciously listening for. There was the sound of a car being driven up the track. It came to a halt, a car door slammed and Christy heard Adam walk into the house.

She expected him to go straight to bed. He must be as tired as she was. He did no such thing. He walked swiftly through the house to the door of her bedroom, swung open the door and switched on the light.

The light hurt her eyes. For a moment Christy couldn't see him. She lay against the pillows, her hand flung up to protect herself from the glare.

'So you're conscious, then.'

It was a voice Christy hadn't heard before, sharp and laced with anger. It made Christy flinch.

'Of. . .of course I'm conscious.'

He walked over to the bed and stood staring down at her. 'What the hell do you think you're playing at?'

'I came home,' Christy said in a small voice. 'I'm allowed to come home.'

'I left instructions that you were to be under observation for twenty-four hours. As soon as my back is turned you're up and out of hospital like. . .like. . .'

'Like I'm fine,' Christy finished for him. 'Adam, I am fine. Honestly. Kate saw me. . .'

'Kate is not your doctor!'

'Who is?' Christy lay back and eyed him hopefully. His anger was almost palpable, like a tightly coiled spring about to be released.

'I was tonight.'

'No.' Christy shook her head decisively and winced

slightly at the movement. 'You handed me over to Kate.' She fingered the dressing at the side of her face. 'And a very neat job she did too.'

Adam stared down at her, his anger still visible. It was almost as if he wanted to hit her — hit something at any rate. Finally he closed his eyes in defeat.

'Well, you have to get up now,' he said flatly.

Christy sat bolt upright, dragging the sheet with her as a sop to modesty. Her nightgown was skimpy to say the least. 'I'm not going back to hospital, Adam McCormack, and you can't make me.' She glared up at him.

'No.' He shook his head and his voice was weary. 'Not the hospital. We need you to go to the pharmacy.'

'The pharmacy. . .' Christy took a deep breath and swallowed, her defiance ebbing. 'What do you need?'

'We've had to do a craniotomy on Mrs Haddon.' He was looking at her now, his eyes not seeing her. 'We've drilled burr holes and alleviated the worst of the pressure.'

'Drill holes!' Any vestige of weariness had slipped from Christy. She stared at Adam in horror. 'A craniotomy, here! With these facilities! Adam!'

'It's not what I would have chosen,' he said grimly. 'There was massive bleeding into the brain. If we'd tried to transfer her. . .'

'She would have died before Melbourne,' Christy agreed. She threw off her sheet, regardless of her skimpy nightgown, crossed to door and retrieved her robe from the hook. 'How can I help?'

Adam looked at her strangely. 'Just like that?'

'Of course "just like that",' Christy said impatiently. 'What do you need, Adam?'

'We haven't enough intravenous antibiotic at the hospital,' he told her. 'If you'd stayed where you were supposed to be, Richard could have taken the pharmacy key and gone himself. He says he knows his way round the pharmacy.'

'Dr Blair can stay out of my pharmacy.' Christy pushed her feet into slippers. 'As can you, Dr McCormack. Heaven knows what you'd end up giving the unfortunate woman. What are you using?'

He told her and she nodded. 'There's plenty at the pharmacy. I'll go now.' Then she paused, frowning. 'My car's still outside Amy Haddon's.'

'I'll drive you down,' Adam said firmly. 'You should be in hospital under observation — not driving around the countryside. Besides, if you think I'm letting you go into a dark pharmacy at midnight you have another think coming.'

'No, Adam,' she said meekly.

He looked at her suspiciously. 'What did you say?'

Christy gave a rueful smile. He really did think she was going to throw his offer of company in his face. He was tired and she didn't want to put him to more trouble but she wanted even less to go into the pharmacy by herself tonight.

'What. . .what have they done to him?' she asked quietly.

Adam was still looking suspicious but at her words his brow cleared. 'If I tell you your attacker's out on bail, will you let me drive you?' he demanded.

'He's not!' Christy said, in horror.

Adam relented. 'He's not,' he admitted. 'Nor is he likely to be for a long time.' He stood at the door, waiting for her to pass. 'But I'm coming with you all the same.'

'Yes, Adam.'

It was a strange night. There was a feeling of unreality about driving through the darkened bush with Adam. Christy hadn't bothered to dress. If she'd been feeling a little less light-headed she might have pulled on a tracksuit but the pain-killers she had taken were having their effect. It would be an effort to dress and she felt like making as little effort as possible.

She was used to night calls back to the pharmacy whenever the doctors required drugs they didn't have on hand, but tonight it was different. The fact that a man such as Amy Haddon's attacker existed changed Christy's perspective of the world. No longer would she be fearless. Dark shadows would stay with her for a very long time.

Adam stood by the dispensary door while she prepared what she needed and she was absurdly comforted by his presence. What was it about this man that made her feel so safe?

Two minutes later they were in the car again, travelling through the darkened town towards the hospital.

'I just need to insert this into the drip,' Adam told her, pulling into the hospital car park. 'I won't be more than a moment.'

'I'll. . . I'll come in with you.' Christy looked down at her nightwear and winced. She should have put on some clothes, but she had expected only to go to the pharmacy. Common sense dictated that she stay in the car now, but the car was dark and so was the car park. With Adam went her security.

'The night staff aren't going to be fussy,' he smiled, his eyes following her gaze and guessing her thoughts. 'Besides, it's a change from your oh, so efficient work clothes.'

'There's nothing wrong with my work clothes,' she said stiffly.

His eyes were still on her. 'I like this better,' he said decisively. He held out a hand to take hers. 'Come on, then, Miss Blair.'

For a moment—just a moment—Christy hesitated, and then the temptation was too much. His hand was strong and warm and commanding. She put out her own and he held it as if it belonged to him. Once again the overpowering feeling of being loved and protected swept over her. If it were only true. . . If only this man had no past haunting him — no one to phone in the middle of the night three thousand miles away. . .

She stood at the door of the intensive care ward as Adam adjusted the drip. As Adam had said, the staff were not concerned with Christy's appearance. They were too concerned with the health of the woman on the bed.

Amy Haddon's head was bandaged with white dressing and her face was almost the same colour as the bandages. She was totally unmoving. Her hands were lying stiffly by her sides where they had been placed. She looked. . . She looked dead, Christy thought miserably. What hope did she have? Had they been in time alleviating the pressure?

Adam finished what he had to do and then stood looking down at Amy for a long moment. Finally he picked up one of her work-worn hands from its rigid position and rubbed it lightly in his.

'You're safe now, Amy,' he said gently and Christy's heart knotted at the gentleness and concern in his voice. 'The man who hurt you has been arrested. You're with friends and you're safe. All you have to do now is get well. All you have to do is wake up. Open your eyes and see us now, Amy.'

The silence stretched on and on. Christy stared at the floor, misery etched on her face. It was all so hopeless. If the lout had hit Amy so hard as to make her bleed into her brain. . .

'Amy. . .' Adam's words went on in the stillness. 'Come on, Amy. It's safe to wake up now. Christy's here. You remember Miss Blair. The lout who hurt you will remember Miss Blair, too. The police tell me Christy kneed him so hard he can't bear to zip his jeans up.'

Despite her misery Christy gave a tiny choke of laughter. If it was really true. . . She had kneed him, she remembered, and she remembered where. The thought gave her a tiny spurt of satisfaction.

She crossed to the bed and touched Amy Haddon lightly on the face. 'I wish I'd hurt him more,' she whispered. 'For your sake. . .'

And then the miracle happened. The dead look lifted imperceptibly as muscles in the woman's face moved. She stirred ever so slightly. Adam's grip on her hand tightened and he spoke again.

'Come on, Amy. You can do it. Open your eyes for us.' He smiled. 'Miss Blair here is wearing a piece of fluff that's worth looking at, if only to note the falling moral standards of the younger generation.' Then, as Christy gave an indignant gasp and clutched the lace at her breast into a more decent position, Amy opened her eyes.

For a moment she didn't see them. She stared straight up, her eyes adjusting sightlessly to the light, and there was fear behind her eyes. Adam let her be for a moment before speaking.

'Amy?' he said softly. 'Welcome back, Amy.'

Was there brain damage? The next few moments would tell. They didn't have to wait that long, though. Amy Haddon's gaze turned towards Adam's voice. His hand gripped hers still, and her face twisted into an attempt to smile.

'Dr McCormack,' she whispered. 'Christy. . .' And she started to cry.

They left her as she drifted into sleep. Her awful pallor had eased, and she lay in natural sleep. The tension in the hospital had eased dramatically.

'She's not out of the woods yet,' Adam warned, as he ushered Christy out to the car. 'But we'll be unlucky if the bleeding causes any more problems.'

Christy sank into his car without a word. In truth she was close to tears herself. The emotions of the night were too much for her to absorb.

Adam too fell silent. He glanced across at her once or twice on the drive back up to their cottage, but didn't speak. There was a tension between them that kept them silent, despite the strong feeling of contentment that Amy's recovery had caused.

Christy walked into the house alone while Adam removed his bag and locked the little car. She stood in the kitchen, irresolute. She should go straight to bed, her head told her, and yet something stronger made her put the kettle on to boil and then stand by the stove and wait for him. He must have stood on the veranda for a while — giving her time to be well out of the kitchen, she thought. She deserved that. She'd been avoiding him and it seemed he was respecting that wish. Now, though. . . Now she stood and told herself she was waiting for the kettle to boil but she was doing no such thing. She was waiting for Adam.

Finally he came, swinging the kitchen door wide and coming silently in as though fearful of disturbing her. When he saw her he stopped dead.

'Not in bed, my Christy?' he said, and his voice was wary.

'No.' Christy fumbled in the overhead cupboard. 'I. . . I'm making myself a cup of tea. I. . .would you like one?'

'No.'

'Oh.' Christy paused, unsure of how to respond. Adam put his medical case against the wall and stood watching her. 'I. . . I guess I'll have one myself, then.'

'Why aren't you running?'

Christy looked across at him. 'I don't. . . I don't know what you mean.'

'You should be in the bedroom with the door locked,' he said grimly. His arms were folded against his chest. He looked stern and forbidding.

'Adam. . .' Christy looked across at him, her eyes pleading for something even she didn't understand. She caught her breath. 'Adam, I'm sorry about your wife.' Her words shocked her. She hadn't meant to say it. It was the wrong time. . .the wrong thing to say. It was utterly inappropriate and yet she had said it as though compelled.

Adam's face was still. He shook his head, as though not wanting her to continue, but Christy had to keep going.

'I found out today. . .about the schizophrenia.'

He frowned. 'You didn't know that?'

She shook her head miserably. 'No one told me,' she whispered. She took a cup down from the shelf and banged it with unnecessary force on the table. 'No one tells me anything.'

'What on earth do you mean by that?' She had Adam's whole attention now. The still, taut look had faded, replaced by something else. He was frowning.

'Meaning no one even told me you had a wife,' Christy burst out. 'No one, Adam McCormack. Do you think I would have let you kiss me all those years ago if I'd thought you had a wife? Adam. . .'

The frown had faded, softening to something approaching laughter. 'Oh, Christy. . .'

'You don't even remember it,' she said savagely. 'Just a kiss. Just a kiss to keep your mind off Sarah. But I wouldn't have. . . I would never have let you kiss me. . .'

'Why not?'

His voice cut across her rising hysteria like a whip. It stopped her dead.

'Because. . .' she said lamely. 'Because I don't kiss married men.'

Adam nodded. He walked over and pulled another cup down, put coffee into both cups and poured water.

'I'm making tea,' Christy said miserably.

'By the time you make tea it'll be morning.' He put down the kettle and turned to face her. 'Christy, I do remember that kiss.'

She bit her lip. 'I shouldn't have said anything,' she said bitterly.

'And I shouldn't have kissed you all those years ago,'

Adam said softly. 'It was true. I didn't have the right. But I was as miserable as all hell and you were young and laughing and loving and. . .and the most desirable woman. . .'

'Not as desirable as Sarah,' Christy interjected.

Adam shook his head. 'By that time I'd lost Sarah,' he said sadly. 'She was either trying to play a role she no longer understood, or she was flat or manic. The time she came. . .the time you met her. . .was one of the final times we had where she was anything approaching normal.' He shook his head. 'She wouldn't take medication. If she approached health, she stopped the medication dead, and then the whole vicious cycle started again. The week I came down with Richard to stay with you I'd accepted that the marriage was effectively over. She'd been near well, but she would have none of ordinary life. When she was well she wanted to be off skiing or dancing or modelling in exotic locations. It was as if she couldn't keep still. So I came on holiday with Richard. And I met you.'

'You didn't remember me,' Christy said bleakly. 'When I met you at the airport. . .'

Adam took her shoulders in his hands, and she could feel the strength of him through the thin lace of her nightgown. 'I did remember you, my Christy. Why do you think I came?'

Christy's world stopped spinning. Her face lost its colour.

'Don't,' she said, and her voice was a thread. 'Don't joke with me, Adam. It's not fair.'

'I'm not joking. I was never more serious about anything in my life.'

She shook her head. 'You didn't recognise me.'

'No.' He smiled down at her. 'I didn't. Not at first.' He touched her hair with his fingers. 'You had black hair when I last saw you. With chestnut highlights, I seem to remember.'

'Black. . .' Christy frowned up at him and then her

eyes creased in sudden laughter. She had too. As a student she had hated being blonde and for a whole three months she had been a stunning brunette. After that she had tried red hair, but after a session with a malevolent bottle of dye that tinged her red with brassy green she had welcomed her blonde hair back with relief. She gave a choked chuckle.

'You really are blonde?' Adam demanded. His hands were back gripping her shoulders again.

'I am.' Christy tried to shake his hands from her shoulders but he didn't move. 'You're crazy, Adam McCormack. How can you say you came all the way to Australia to see a woman you hadn't seen for five years? I'm not the same Christy Blair. My hair has changed. I'm no longer a student. Everything has changed.'

'No.'

She looked up, her brow creased, and found Adam's dark eyes smiling down at her. Her heart lurched and she twisted in his grasp. 'What. . .what hasn't changed?' she asked breathlessly.

'This.' He bent his head and kissed her.

This time it was right. This time was the best. This was the moment Christy had waited for all her life.

There were still unanswered questions. They didn't matter now. The questions could wait. Adam said he had remembered her for those five long years, and she believed him. For tonight at least she believed him. She was incapable of doing anything else.

She kissed him with a passion that matched his own, entwining her arms around his head and pulling him into her, deepening the kiss. The coffee grew cold on the table beside them but neither noticed. All that mattered was each other.

Adam held her to him as if he would never let her go. His hands held the slim contours of her body against his, feeling the curves of her waist through the

soft fabric of her gown. His mouth enveloped her, his
tongue seeking knowledge of her. He wanted her.

Christy could feel his burning need, and she gloried
in it. Her body was doing strange things. She pressed
herself closer, closer, trying to assuage the fire growing
within — a fire she had never felt before and didn't fully
understand. She only knew that the fire was for Adam.

His hands stroked her as she pressed closer. Christy's
lips tasted him and her tongue did its own exploration
of the salt of his mouth — the broad expanse of teeth
and tongue. Dear God, she wanted him. This was the
man she had wanted for five long years and her
imagination had not played her false. She had known
he would feel like this. She had known she wanted
him. She ran her hands through his coarse, unruly hair
and a groan broke from him. He pulled back to stare
at her.

'Christy. . .' It was a caress. It was a declaration of
love. It was all Christy could ever need. Love and
desire and tenderness were mixed in that word and she
smiled shyly up at him.

'Adam?'

He put his hand down to the soft curve where the
lace of her nightgown covered her breasts. Tiny pearl
buttons hid her from him. Carefully he loosened each
button in turn, as if handling something of infinite
value. Then, slowly, he lifted her gown back from her
shoulders. It dropped unheeded to the floor.

She was naked. Apart from the incongruous dressing
on the side of her face, Christy was naked. She had
never been before a man naked in her life, but she
wasn't shy. She wanted Adam to see her. She belonged
to him as surely as he belonged to her. She looked up
and smiled gently at him.

'I love you, Adam McCormack,' she said softly.

He touched the dressing on her face softly with his
finger, and then his hand moved to cup her breast.

'You are so lovely, my Christy. I have dreamed of you for so long. . .'

It wasn't true. It couldn't be true, but for the moment Christy wasn't questioning Adam's words. She reached forward and undid the buttons of his shirt, and then slid a hand in to feel the coarse hair of his chest. It felt good. It felt right.

And then he was gathering her naked body into him, holding her to him as if he could never let her go. His hands slid over the smooth satin of her skin, running from shoulder around to breast and then down to thigh. Christy gasped with pleasure as she felt where his hands were searching. Her body arched against him. Closer. Closer. Her body was screaming at her, the fire consuming her thighs — her breast — her very being.

Then somehow Adam was lifing her, cradling her to him, kissing her deeply as he moved into her bedroom. The big bed received her softly and he stood above her, looking down in the moonlight.

'Christy. . .' His voice was uncertain. 'Christy, my love. . .'

She reached up to take his hands, drawing him down to kiss his lips. It was she who was sure now. It was she who knew what must happen.

'I want you, Adam,' she whispered. 'I want you more than life itself. Adam. . .'

Somehow he drew away. For a long moment he stood looking down at the soft sheen of her skin in the dim light. He reached down and ran a hand from the hollow of her throat, around the swell of her breasts, then down across the flatness of her belly and into the welcoming moistness of her thighs. 'Are you sure, my Christy?'

For answer she arched herself up, her thighs closing on his hand. 'Adam,' she whispered, and he could hear the fire in her voice. 'Adam. . .'

'Wait,' he said. He bent again and kissed her hard

on the lips, and his hand withdrew from where she most wanted it to be. 'Wait, my Christy.' And he was gone.

A moment later he returned. Christy had lain unmoving, waiting for her man. Her body was alive to him, aflame, waiting for a consummation that had waited five long years. Then, as Adam appeared, her eyes widened at the sight of him. His nakedness awed her. He was. . .he was magnificent. With one lithe movement she rose and met him, her naked skin closing on his in joy. This was right. This was her place. This was her Adam.

And then he lifted her triumphantly into his arms, claiming her as his own. As he lowered her on to the bed he came too, skin against skin, two bodies merging into a power of passion that could know no equal. Christy arched herself closer, closer and then as the pain came as she had known it must she cried out in ecstasy. It was the fulfilment of a perfect dream. The pain faded as the rhythm of the night took over. Adam loved her as she had known he would. The night merged into a glory of stars and light and joy as they became one.

CHAPTER NINE

CHRISTY slept that night as she had not slept since she was a child. In Adam's arms she drifted into unconsciousness, the events of the night and Adam's love combining to make her exhausted, loved and safe. She didn't stir.

Just before dawn the telephone rang and he rose, gently disentangling her from his arms. She stirred but didn't wake. Her dreams were too lovely.

He returned an hour later to find her still asleep, but as he opened the bedroom door she stirred to wakefulness. 'Adam?' she said drowsily.

'Go back to sleep, my love,' he said tenderly. He crossed to the bed and looked down at her curled form. She looked young and defenceless in the big bed, with the white dressing over the side of her face. Despite her bruises she looked incredibly lovely. He bent and kissed her on the dressing.

'Where have you been?' She stirred languorously in the bed, reluctant to allow the day to begin.

'Delivering babies,' he said solemnly.

'Babies. . .'

'Yep.' He sat on the bed and grinned happily down at her. 'Two of 'em. Mrs Fry had twin daughters, four weeks premature.' He shook his head. 'Richard hadn't diagnosed them. I've left the Frys in shock, wondering how they're going to make three dozen nappies go the distance.'

'The babies are OK?' Christy struggled to a sitting position. The sheet fell to her waist, and, suddenly shy, she seized it and pulled it modestly up to her shoulders. Adam's grin broadened.

'They're healthy and perfect,' he told her. 'Heaven

115

help Mrs Fry if they'd gone to term. They were six pounds apiece as it was. I'm sorry I disturbed you. You need to sleep.'

Christy's gaze fell to her bedside clock and her eyes widened. 'Eight-thirty!' she squeaked. She threw back the sheet and then made a grab for her discarded robe as she remembered her nakedness. With a swift movement Adam lifted the robe up and away from her.

'Why bother?' he asked. 'It's a warm morning.'

'Adam, give me back my robe,' she gasped. 'I have to be at work by nine.'

'No,' he said solidly.

'No?' Christy stopped, bemused. She made another grab for her robe but he stepped back. Defeated, she dropped back into bed and drew up the covers. 'It's Saturday,' she said. 'The pharmacy opens on Saturday morning.'

'Not this morning,' Adam told her. 'As we speak Ruth is putting a very large notice on the pharmacy door, saying that, due to extreme heroism and a bump on the head on the part of the pharmacist, the pharmacy will open only for emergency scripts this morning. I'm not giving out any emergency scripts. Richard's under orders, so barring snake bites or other unexpected dramas you have the day off.'

'I don't think I have a lot for snake bite anyway,' Christy said doubtfully. She looked up at him. 'I can work. . .'

'You're not going to.' He placed his hands firmly on her shoulders and pushed her back on to the pillows. 'You disobeyed my orders last night. You will obey them now.'

'I'm not very good at taking orders,' she confessed. 'I'm better at giving them.'

Adam grinned. 'It's grounds for incompatibility.' He touched her face lightly and his smile faded. 'Christy, last night. . .' He hesitated. 'It was your first time?'

'Yes,' she said shyly.

The next question was left hanging in the air. Why? Adam should have said, and Christy would have told him. I was waiting for you. The question and answer lay unspoken between them. If they had been uttered the commitment would be absolute.

Christy's commitment was absolute anyway. She looked up at Adam and her heart twisted in love. She could never be more in love than she was at this moment. She took his hand between hers and held it to her cheek. 'It was worth waiting for,' she said lightly, and she smiled against his hand. 'I'm glad you had the forethought to take precautions.'

'No babies?' He sank down on to the bed. 'I would have thought you were more aware of the dangers, with your attitude to motherhood.'

'My attitude. . .' Christy frowned and then remembered what she had told him. She had told him she didn't want children. It was hardly appropriate to set him right now — to tell him that she could imagine no greater joy than to have his children. She made herself smile and turn the moment into laughter.

'What size was it?'

His brows drew together as he met her look. Christy's eyes were dancing up at him. 'I beg your pardon?'

'What you used last night. What size was it?' And then at Adam's look Christy chuckled. 'We sell them at the pharmacy,' she told him. 'As a joke Ruth put them into three boxes. She labelled them standard, large and extra large. The large haven't been touched. Every woman who buys them for her husband goes straight to the standard box and every man who buys them goes straight to the extra large. We haven't failed yet.'

Adam choked. 'Miss Blair!' he said in shocked tones. 'I can't believe I'm hearing right.'

'I wouldn't tell you this if you weren't a doctor,' she smiled. 'I'm speaking as one professional to another.'

'Of course,' he agreed gravely and then laughed again. He sounded young, Christy thought. Young and happy. He sounded younger than she had ever heard him before.

She placed a finger up to touch the nape of his neck where the collar of his short-sleeved shirt met the tanned skin of his broad neck. 'Adam?'

He leaned back against her. 'You should be asleep.'

'I. . . I don't think I can sleep.'

'Oh.' He appeared to give the matter serious consideration. 'Ruth's put the notice up,' he said at last. 'It seems a pity to waste it.'

'I should go to work.'

'Nope.' He turned to her then and lifted the sheet from her grasp, allowing it to fall to her waist. 'Are you sure you can't sleep?' he asked.

'S-sure.' His eyes were caressing her and Christy was suddenly breathless.

'Then what you need, my lady,' he said, running his finger down the smooth curve of her skin, 'is occupational therapy. Something to keep your mind off your sore head.'

'Oh,' Christy said blankly. Her body was alight to his touch and she was having trouble thinking of anything but the passage of his hand down her body. 'Can you. . .can you think of anything that might work?'

'I have just the therapy,' he told her.

Afterwards Adam slept again, but Christy lay wakeful in his arms. She was sated with love and happiness. She had slept her fill. To sleep more would be to waste the moment — to squander this absolute joy in sleep. She lay in his arms and listened to the cockatoos squawking in the gums outside the house and was content. There were problems. She knew there would be problems but there was nothing they couldn't sort out. Not now. Not now they had acknowledged their love.

'He hasn't told me he loves me,' she whispered into the morning light. 'But he will. He does.' She stirred slightly, savouring the feel of his chest curved around the small of her back. This was where she belonged. This was her home.

The phone rang half an hour later, and this time it was Christy who answered it, rising swiftly to lift the receiver before Adam woke. He stirred but as the sound of the phone cut off he drifted back into sleep.

'Christy, it's Richard,' her brother said apologetically. 'Did I wake you?'

'No.'

'Sorry to drag you out but I need a ventolin pump,' he told her. 'I have a little boy here who's been visiting his aunt and goes home today. I don't want to send him off without a pump.'

'I'll be at the pharmacy in fifteen minutes,' she told him.

'Thank you.' He hesitated. 'Christy, Kate tells me things are difficult between you and Adam.'

'I wouldn't worry,' she said gently. She looked through the bedroom door at Adam's sleeping form. 'We're working it out.'

It was a swift trip down to the pharmacy. She pulled on shorts and blouse, deciding that if she looked professional and open for business she might not be able to leave the shop again. She sold the pump to the child's aunt and reinforced Richard's lesson in how to use it.

'You have to make sure it goes all the way down,' she told the little boy. 'The mixture doesn't do anything unless it goes much further than your mouth. What's your favourite football team?'

'Essendon, of course,' Jamie told her.

'OK.' Christy smiled. 'Imagine the stuff in this little machine is red and black stripes. I want you to get yourself red and black striped lungs every time you use the pump, and your lungs are right down here. Footballers need good lungs.'

'I'll never be a footballer,' the little boy said sadly.

'Why ever not?' Christy sat back on her heels and gazed at him.

''Cos I'm an asthmatic.'

Christy shook her head. 'Not a problem,' she said soundly. She stood up and fetched a small book from a display rack near them. 'Here's a present. It's a book telling you all about asthma and at the back it tells you all the famous sportsmen and women who have asthma.'

'Even some footballers?' Jamie said suspiciously.

'Cross my heart and hope to break a leg,' she said firmly.

She smiled as she waved the little boy off. She'd just lost any profit she might make from the nebuliser sale by giving away the book, but it was worth it. She felt great this morning, so why shouldn't Jamie?

She let herself back into the house quietly. Adam was still alseep. Christy thought of the look of strain he had carried since he'd arrived in Australia and her heart went out to him. He seemed to need sleep more than she did. Whatever had happened over the last few years with Sarah must have been dreadful.

Breakfast. All of a sudden she was starving. What had happened to dinner last night? She shrugged. Last night's dinner was a meal lost, and all of a sudden she was missing it.

And she could cook for two. Three! From the window-ledge Charlie watched with hopeful eyes. She turned on the radio and sang silently along as she made eggs and bacon, hot buttered toast and percolated coffee. She ate as if she hadn't eaten for months, fed Charlie, and then she made up a tray for Adam. When she opened the bedroom door he was wide awake, waiting for her.

'About time, too,' he grinned. 'The smells have been driving me nuts for fifteen minutes.'

Christy smiled down at him. 'What a way to greet breakfast in bed. Aren't you grateful?'

'I'm grateful.' He sat up with alacrity and fixed her with a look. 'Have you eaten?'

'Of course.'

'I suspected as much. Now the natural order of things. . .'

'Is women and children first,' Christy finished serenely. 'And I'm still hungry, Adam McCormack, so I'd better have some grovelling gratitude right now or I'll scoff the lot. Especially as the agreement was for the landlady to have breakfast in bed.'

'It was too,' Adam said contritely. 'I tell you what. I'll finish this, then you hop back into bed and I'll make lunch.'

'Adam McCormack. . .'

'You're not supposed to say "Adam McCormack" when being given orders,' he told her, between mouthfuls of bacon. 'I'm used to people saying "Yes, Doctor". I like it,' he grinned. 'You should try it.'

'It'd choke me.' Christy walked over to the door.

'Where do you think you're going?' he said direfully. 'You're an invalid, Christy Blair. Your place is in bed.'

'Not with toast crumbs, it's not,' Christy laughed. 'I'm going to have a shower.'

'Don't get your stitches wet,' Adam told her.

Christy stopped, frowning. 'Can't I get them wet?' she asked. 'How can I shower, then?'

'Wait until I finish my breakfast and I'll come and hold the umbrella,' he grinned, and then ducked as the cushion from the chair beside the door came hurtling across the room at him. 'If you're not sleeping, then how about a picnic? All I need to make me a happy man is a large tree, some grass and preferably some swimable water.' He smiled across at her, and his look turned her legs to jelly. 'And you, my love,' he said softly.

Christy smiled back at him, lost in the caress his eyes were giving her. 'I know the perfect place,' she said, and then hesitated. 'But can I swim?'

'Doesn't Blair Pharmacy run to bathing caps?' The warmth in Adam's eyes deepened and spread into every part of her. 'Or maybe you can float with your head on my chest. I can't imagine any load I'd rather bear.'

'I. . .' Christy had trouble finding her voice. When she did it didn't sound right. 'I'll fetch a bathing cap,' she said unsteadily.

It was a lovely, aimless day. The tensions of the past few weeks had lifted as if they had never been, and the medical demands were, for once, few. Their sickest patient, Amy, was transferred mid-morning via ambulance to Melbourne. 'The bleeding seems to be stabilised,' Adam told Christy. 'And I want an orthopaedic surgeon to set that arm.' The newly arrived twins settled down to enjoy the fussing of the nursing staff and Adam was free.

Four miles from town the river ran through the property of one of Christy's elderly customers who'd told her she could swim there whenever she wished. It was an idyllic spot, the river running along a sandy bank at the foot of a heavily wooded valley. There was a maidenhair fern growing thickly under the gums, making a soft bed on which they lay. They rested and talked of everything that didn't matter, then swam, ate their sandwiches, drank wine, made love and finally slept under the canopy of the eucalypts, the mobile phone in the picnic basket staying blessedly quiet.

They woke as the sun dipped across the horizon.

'Do we have to go home?' Christy asked sadly. This was like time out. It was too perfect. Soon something

would burst her lovely bubble and she would go back
to the desolation she had known before. For now. . .
For now Adam was before her, his body gleaming and
muscled, his smile warming her and loving her.

He took her in his arms and kissed her, and then
held her back at arm's length. 'You are the most
beautiful woman, Christy Blair. You almost make
me. . .'

'Make you what?' Christy said gently. She had felt
him bring himself up sharply, as if he had remembered
something he would rather forget. 'Make you what?'

He shook his head, and his eyes lost a little of their
laughter. 'Make me young again,' he said, and Christy
knew it hadn't been that at all.

She leaned forward into his arms. 'Quoth the grey
beard,' she said lightly. 'How old are you, Adam
McCormack?'

'Far too old for you,' he smiled, but his smile didn't
reach his eyes.

'Thirty-two?' she guessed. 'Thirty-three? Oh,
ancient! That's only seven years older than me, Adam.'
She lifted her face to be kissed. 'And I have a distinct
preference for older men. At least,' she added truth-
fully, 'for one older man.'

She couldn't say more than that. She was throwing
herself at him now but she no longer cared. She was
Adam's. She would have Adam McCormack on any
terms he cared to name. She loved him and love had
no pride, at least not where Christy was concerned.

He kissed her then, but his kiss was not as deep.
There was a shadow between them. 'We'll have
another swim before we go,' he said lightly, and he
turned away, diving swiftly into the river behind him.

Christy didn't join him. She sat on the bank and
watched his muscled body cutting through the water.
He swam from one curve in the river to another and
then back again, over and over, his arms slicing through
the clear water with strength and skill. He didn't let

up. She sat there as the sunset deepened to dusk, watching him swim and wondering just what demons were driving Adam McCormack.

Finally he had to stop. He pulled himself from the water and towelled himself dry. Still the telephone remained silent and Christy blessed her luck. As Adam dried himself she sat looking over the darkening river. Without looking up she said gently, 'Tell me about, Sarah, Adam.'

She had thought he wouldn't tell her. She had expected him to withdraw as he had in the past and for a moment she was sure of it as the silence stretched on and on. Then Adam gave a sigh and came to stand beside her. He picked up a branch near where she sat and started breaking pieces off to throw into the river. It seemed as if the task took all his concentration. He couldn't look at Christy.

'Sarah was my wife and I loved her,' he said, and his voice was harsh with memory. 'But she died a long time ago.'

'It was only six months. . .'

'I know.' Once again the voice was dull with pain. 'Sarah committed suicide six months ago. Oh, the police put it down as an accident, but Sarah took my car keys while I slept and drove my car at full speed into a massive tree. It was no accident.'

'She. . .she was still living with you. . .'

'No.' Adam shook his head. 'It's hard to describe what it was like,' he told her. 'Sarah lived mainly in institutions for the last few years of her life. She wouldn't. . .just wouldn't take her medication unless forced. She was convinced she could become well by herself — that what was wrong with her was a figment of everyone else's imagination. Sarah's demons were real. It was everyone else who had the problem in that we hadn't seen them.'

'But she was with you when she died.'

'Yes.' Adam paused in his repetitive snapping of the

twigs. He turned to Christy and his face in the dusk was bleak with despair. 'I hated seeing her in the institution,' he said. 'They gave her too much medication. They had to, I guess, or she never would have stayed there, and out of the place she was manic. I went to see her and she pleaded with me to take her out. I took a week's leave to take care of her.' He shrugged. 'I was a fool to try. On the second morning of her stay I woke to find her gone. Half an hour later the police told me the car had been crashed.'

'Oh, Adam.' Christy stood and placed a hand gently in his.

'So you see. . .' Adam pulled away '. . .I might be only nine years older than you, Christy, but I feel about a hundred. Now, shall we pack up these picnic things?'

Christy looked at his turned back, biting her lip. It was as if he was rejecting her. Maybe he was. . .

And then he turned and held out his hand. 'Come on, Christy, love,' he smiled. 'I have to do a ward-round including my new twins before bedtime.'

'Bedtime,' Christy said softly and smiled.

Adam's smile faded. 'Christy, I. . . What we're doing. . . Christy, I thought I could block out the past. . .'

Christy shook her head. 'You can't, Adam,' she said firmly. 'You shouldn't even try.' She stood on her toes to kiss him. 'I know you have ghosts, but I can wait until you're free of them. I can wait for a very long time.'

'You might have to,' he said under his breath.

They slept in each other's arms again that night but it was different. Something had changed. Christy lay and stared into the dark, listening to her nightjars and trying to analyse it.

It was as if the night before had been a declaration of their love but the day had brought wiser counsel to Adam. He still wanted her. His eyes caressed her. His smile warmed her and his whole being told her that she was desirable and desired.

So what was different? It was as if now he was making love to her against his better judgement. He was looking at her as he would look at something precious which he was going to lose. Something which was his only on loan until circumstances snatched it away.

Maybe that was Sarah's legacy, Christy decided. Maybe losing Sarah to such an insidious disease had left him with a disbelief in permanence. How would she feel if such a thing happened to her — if someone she loved became someone she didn't know through mental disease?

It didn't bear thinking about. She moved her body closer to Adam's, trying to impart comfort with her presence. Maybe in time. . .

She had waited five years for this man. She could wait for longer, especially if that waiting was by his side.

An hour later the phone rang. Christy half woke as Adam left her. She lay in the dark, waiting for him to return, or for the sound of the car as he was called out. Neither happened and as Christy woke fully she recognised the change in the tone of Adam's voice. He wasn't talking to a patient. She knew by his voice that he was talking to someone he knew and loved. He was talking to someone back home in England.

The temptation to rise and listen by the door was almost overwhelming but Christy bit it back hard. It was Adam's business and Adam had a right to privacy.

Has he a right to make love to me and then speak like that to another woman? she demanded of herself. Adam obviously thought he did. Christy closed her eyes, squeezing back the tears. She was fighting for Adam but she didn't know what she was fighting against. How could he make the decision to come here when he had ties back home?

Then his voice changed. There was anger in his tone now, and impatience. Once again Christy shoved the pillow over her head and tried to ignore it. Whatever it was — whoever it was — Adam had elected to come to Australia. Adam had chosen to come to her.

What she wanted to do more than anything else in the world was to walk into the living-room, take a sharp pair of scissors and cut through the telephone cord. Cut off the ghosts, she thought grimly. If only it were that easy.

The phone call ended. She stirred restlessly in her bed, waiting for him to return. She heard him go into the kitchen and she heard the sounds of tea being made. She waited.

Half an hour later she realised that he was not returning. He had gone back to bed in his own room — at the other end of the house.

The following morning Adam woke her. Christy had slept fitfully after he had left, but towards dawn had fallen into a deeper sleep. She woke as he appeared at the door, breakfast tray in hand.

'I thought it was about time I paid the rent,' he smiled. He placed the tray on the bedside table and bent to kiss her gently on the lips.

It seemed the ghosts were back where they belonged. Christy sat up sleepily, warmed and reassured by his smile. No man could talk to a lover in England hours before and then smile at a woman like that. Or could he?

It didn't matter. Once again she reassured herself. Adam is here, and I'm here. Nothing else matters.

'You left me,' she said, keeping her voice light.

'You were snoring,' he told her, crossing to pull back the curtains and let the morning sun stream on to the bed.

'I never snore,' Christy gasped. She vented her indignation on a piece of toast and regarded her teeth marks with satisfaction. She glared up at Adam, pleased that he'd given her an excuse to sound angry.

'You don't need to take it personally,' Adam said kindly. 'It's only vibration of the soft palate.'

'I don't snore and my soft palate doesn't vibrate, Adam McCormack.' Christy bit her toast again and took a mouthful of coffee. 'Especially when I'm wide awake. Which I was when you left, Adam.'

He nodded slowly and then turned to gaze out of the window to the bush below the house. 'Well, let's just say I had some thinking to do.'

'Which you couldn't do with me beside you.'

He turned then and the trouble behind his eyes faded. 'You may have a very rigid soft palate, Miss Blair,' he said softly. 'But you also have a very distracting personality.'

She smiled up at him. It was a lovely day, and Adam was smiling at her as if he loved her. Nothing else could matter.

'How about a picnic lunch down by the river?' she said happily. 'We could swim again.'

He shook his head regretfully. 'I can't, Christy. I've agreed to be on call today and give Richard the day off.'

'But it's Sunday.' Christy frowned. 'We can take the mobile phone after you've done a ward-round.'

'I have to see Bella's husband.'

Christy's frown deepened. 'The real-estate agent.'

Adam nodded.

'But why?' Christy took another mouthful of coffee but it had lost its flavour. 'Are you. . .are you thinking of buying something?'

'Not yet,' Adam told her and his smile was still gentle and warm. 'When I moved in here I was told there was a house for rent becoming available soon. On Friday I learned it was empty.'

'You don't. . .you don't want to stay with me?'

Christy heard the emotion in her voice with horror.

She was exposed now. She was more exposed than she had ever been in her life. All her love and her commitment to this man was in those few words. Where was her pride? She didn't have any, she thought sadly. She never had where Adam was concerned.

Silence. Christy stared into her coffee, her mouth dry. She looked up at Adam and her pain must have been reflected in her eyes, because he made an involuntary movement towards her. He lifted the coffee from her grasp and laid the mug on the bedside table, then took her hands in his.

'Christy, I have to do this,' he said gently. 'I've been thinking things through all night and this is the only way.'

'The only way. . .'

'It would be easy to drift,' he told her. 'There is nothing I would like better than to stay here, make love to you, love you and drift into a long-term relationship. But we have to be sure. . .'

'And you're not?' Christy whispered. She pulled her hands back from his but his grip tightened.

'I'm not,' he told her. 'And I don't think you are either, Christy.' Then as she looked up at him in hurt surprise he gave a grim laugh. 'I know,' he said bitterly. 'You think you are. You. . .you are the sweetest, loveliest thing that has happened to me for a very long time, Christy Blair. You offer me your love without questions. You give me yourself with trust.' He shook his head. 'You're very young, my Christy.'

'I'm not a child,' Christy said, and her words sounded harsh. 'I'm a woman and I'm in love with you.' She twisted her hands and this time she was released. Sliding out of bed, she crossed to the window to stare bleakly out over the valley. 'Adam, I don't understand. . . All I understand is that you have the power to hurt me as no one else can.' She took a deep breath. 'I fell in love with you five years ago. Five years, Adam

McCormack. And I've held you in my heart since then.'

He crossed the room and placed his hands on her shoulders. 'You haven't held me,' he said gently. 'You've held some romantic ideal. The real Adam McCormack. . .well, the real Adam comes from the real world. He doesn't come to you young and innocent and unscarred. Christy, I need us to get some distance. I need you to see me as I really am before I let you commit yourself to me.'

'That's just an excuse.' Anger was clawing at her now. She had opened her heart to a man for the first time in her life. She had offered herself to him and he was saying wait. Wait? For what? For him to find out about this ghost? This woman in England?

Was he playing games with her? He said he had come here because he remembered her, but those phone calls. . . Was he trying to persuade someone to join him? He made love to Christy but he phoned England. He wanted a woman. If the woman in England wouldn't join him then Christy would do.

She felt tears sliding down her cheeks and brushed them away angrily with the back of her hand. What she was doing was crazy. He had hurt her and he would hurt her again. Damn him. Damn him for ever walking into her life.

'You'd better go, then,' she said dully.

'Christy. . .'

'Don't make it any harder than it is,' she whispered. She turned then, and he was close, so close that her face brushed his shoulder as she swung around. 'You knew I loved you when you came,' she said bitterly. 'You knew I fell in love with you five years ago. Well, here I am, still just as naïve, still falling into your arms. Still taking what you're content to give from the scraps of your other life. Well, Adam, I might be stupid but I'm not going to sit back and take it any longer. I want you. I want your love but I'm not content to take someone else's leavings. When you can come to me and say your other life is over. . .that you are free absolutely of ties from the past. . .then if you want me I'll be here. . .' She choked on a sob. Adam made a move to take her in his arms but she warded him off and backed away. 'But until then. . . Until then you can stay out of my life, Adam McCormack. . .'

Adam was watching her, his eyes deep and unfathomable.

'I'm always going to be tied to the past,' he said slowly. 'You can't escape the past.'

'I can cope with memories,' Christy said harshly. 'Memories, photographs, portraits. But not ghosts, Adam McCormack. Not ghosts that telephone you at midnight and make you speak —— ' She broke off and shook her head blindly. 'You'd better go, Adam. You're right. You'd better find somewhere else to live.'

CHAPTER TEN

HE MOVED out that afternoon. Christy spent the afternoon down by the river, avoiding the sight of Adam
gathering his things and moving them to the cottage
further into town. It was a bleak little cottage only a
couple of doors from Amy Haddon's home and Christy
would dearly have liked to fuss a little — clean for him
and fill the place with flowers and a few creature
comforts. Her pride, dormant for so long, rose to
prevent her.

'He can't have it both ways,' she whispered to
herself, floating on her back in the still river water. She
looked up through the canopy of gum leaves, trying to
find the peace that she usually found here. It wasn't to
be found.

Finally she swam slowly to shore and tried to sleep.
Her body was hurting with the pain from the bruises
inflicted on Friday night. Yesterday. . .yesterday she
had been happy and the bruises had been forgotten.
Now they ached unmercifully and the abrasion on the
side of her face throbbed all the time.

So now what? She dried herself and stared out over
the river, searching for answers on its still surface. If
she had relented she could be with Adam now. She
could be down in his little cottage, helping him unpack,
maybe sharing an evening meal with him. And afterwards. . . Afterwards they could make love. . .

'And it wouldn't mean a thing,' she said bitterly to
herself. Making love to Adam was Christy's ultimate
commitment but Adam obviously didn't see it that
way. He needed some space. . . Some space so that he
could phone his love in privacy.

Christy picked up a rock and hurled it into the water

with force. Its impact gave her a momentary spurt of satisfaction and she picked up another. This time, though, she didn't throw it. She couldn't sustain her anger. There was only bleak misery.

Somehow Christy survived the next few days. She hardly saw Adam, which made it easier, although the sight of his name at the bottom of his scripts made her feel odd. It was as if he was part of her life whether she liked it or not. She could avoid him but he was still there.

Amy Haddon was transferred back to Corrook the following weekend. Christy spent Saturday afternoon with her, dismayed to find that the woman hadn't had a visitor since she'd returned two days before.

'It's because they think I'm a drug addict,' Amy said miserably. 'This town judges harshly. They reckon I brought what happened on to myself.'

'That's nonsense,' Christy said solidly. She took Amy's good hand and gripped it hard. 'Addiction can happen to anyone if the circumstances are against them.'

'I know.' Amy lay back against her pillows and blinked back a tear. 'But they don't know it. They think I'm some sort of criminal. I was so lonely before, and now. . .now it's worse.'

'Well, you have one friend,' Christy said firmly. 'And that's me.'

Her heart was torn over the woman's plight. There was little she could do about the town's attitude towards Amy Haddon, though, and she hated to think what harm further isolation would do to her. She walked out of the ward to see Adam striding towards her.

It was the first time in days that they had met face to face. Christy's first impulse was to turn in the other direction but that was crazy. She wanted to leave and the hospital entrance was behind him. She took a deep breath and kept walking.

'Been visiting Amy?' he said quietly. He was wearing his white coat, with his stethoscope swinging from his pocket. He looked professional, calm and detached. He didn't smile. His eyes were cool and appraising.

'Yes.' Christy hesitated, but then made herself speak. Amy would have no one else to intercede on her behalf. 'When can she go home, Adam?'

'She could go home now if I thought she had someone to look after her,' he said calmly. He frowned. 'But she hasn't.'

'She could stay with me.' Christy met his look. 'I have a spare bedroom.'

'I know,' Adam said grimly. He shook his head. 'The Christy Blair speciality. Love and a home for the walking wounded.' He shrugged. 'It wouldn't work with Amy either, Christy. You're away all day, and it's not a long-term solution. She's better staying here until she's physically well enough to cope with isolation.'

'When will that be?' Christy said bleakly.

Adam sighed and Christy noted the deep lines of fatigue around his eyes. The man looked as though he was under almost intolerable strain. It was with a real effort that she stopped herself reaching up to smooth away those lines with her fingers.

'Friday,' Adam said. 'You're right in that she won't be able to cope with the isolation, but at least she'll be as well as we can make her.'

'You haven't. . .you haven't heard from her son?' Christy asked.

'Yes.'

Christy's eyes widened. The word had been harsh and angry. 'You located him?'

'We located him.' Adam put his hands deep into his coat pockets and glared at a spot somewhere just behind Christy's head. 'I put Bella on the job. She found an address and telephone number and I phoned yesterday.'

'And?'

'And he doesn't want to know,' he told her. 'He's married. His wife answered the phone. She said Tom had been hurt too much in the past and didn't want anything to do with his mother.'

'But. . .'

'There's nothing there, Christy.' Adam shrugged. 'You can't blame him. According to Bella, Amy's husband was violent most of the time. He gave Amy a dreadful time but for some unknown reason she stuck to him. She stood between Tom and his father over and over again and Tom has reacted by rejecting them both.' He shrugged again. 'She paid for her husband's violence then and she's paying for it now.'

'Oh, Adam. . .'

His face closed as though her soft ejaculation physically hurt. 'If there's nothing more, Miss Blair. . .'

'There's nothing more,' she said bleakly.

He touched her lightly on the side of the face as though he couldn't help himself. 'Can I. . .? Would you like me to take these stitches out?'

'No, thank you, Dr McCormack,' Christy managed. 'Kate's my doctor.

Amy's isolation stayed in Christy's mind all week. She used the problem to fill the corners of her mind that would otherwise be taken by Adam. She couldn't bear this cold formality. As self-protection she thought of Amy.

A tiny part of a solution came into the pharmacy on the Friday that Amy left hospital—at least he didn't come in but was left in a bag in his owner's car while his owner sought advice.

'I want some worming syrup for some pups,' Matthew Hearn told Christy. 'I dunno what to give these. They're my wife's bitch's litter. When my farm bitch has pups you can shove 'em on the sheep's scale and measure a dose, but these bloody things — they're too small to register.' The farmer shoved his hands in his pockets and looked uncomfortable.

'What sort of dog are they?' Christy asked curiously.

'You tell me and we'll both know,' the farmer said glumly. 'The bitch is part poodle, but the thing I saw sniffing round when she was on heat was a real Heinz fifty-seven varieties.' He glowered. 'And the wife's gone to visit her sister in town and she rings me up and tells me to worm 'em. So tell me what to do.'

Christy smiled. She picked up a bottle of worming syrup. '1.5ml for every 1kg bodyweight,' she read.

'1kg. . .new-fangled damned measurements,' the farmer growled. 'How the heck do I figure that? Lowest weight on the shed scales is 10 kg and the cooking scales are in pounds and ounces.'

The pharmacy was quiet and Christy was intrigued. 'Tell you what,' she offered. 'I've an old scale out the back. I'll weigh them for you. Bring them round through the back lane, though. It'd be my luck to have a health inspector visit just as you carry them through the front door.'

She set up her scale on the back step of the pharmacy, leading down to the service lane. She just had it organised when Matthew appeared, carrying one wriggling, writhing sack.

'How many do you have?' Christy asked, fascinated.

'Only two,' Matthew grunted, putting the sack down with care. 'Two too many if you ask me. And now the wife says she wants to keep one because they're so cute.' He put a large hand into the sack and withdrew two wriggling, writhing, wide-eyed and slightly moist puppies.

Christy could see Mrs Hearn's reasons for wanting to keep one. The puppies were lovely. They gazed around with awe. The smallest gave a tiny, indignant woof and then waved its curly tail like a flag. Its tongue went out in automatic lick mode. Christy found herself laughing for the first time for two weeks.

'Oh, Matthew. They're lovely.' She picked up a squirming fluff bundle and held it to her cheek.

'They'll be useless with sheep,' the farmer said morosely. 'The wife likes 'em, though.'

'They'll be lovely companions,' Christy agreed, and then stopped short. 'Matthew, are you looking for a home for one?'

'Too right,' he said quickly. 'If I keep both much longer the wife'll want both.'

'Amy Haddon would love one of these,' Christy said softly. She looked up at the farmer. 'Amy comes home from hospital today.'

The farmer's face closed. 'Amy Haddon,' he said slowly. 'She's been in trouble with the cops.'

'You know her?' Christy asked, watching his face.

'I went to school with her.' He sighed. 'She was all right until she married Bill Haddon.'

'Matthew, she's still all right,' Christy said gently. 'She's just got herself into a hole of loneliness and depression that's almost impossible for her to get out of.' She placed her wriggling bundle on the scale, carefully noting his weight. 'This little one. . .' She gestured to the pup '. . .might just make that hole a little shallower.'

The farmer considered. He sniffed and looked up to the sky as though trying to find an answer. Finally he nodded.

'OK, Miss Blair,' he said. 'The pup's hers. Dunno what the wife'll say. She's been pretty snippy about Amy Haddon.'

As had most of the ladies of Corrook, Christy thought sadly. Married to a good, kind-hearted husband like Matthew Hearn, Edith Hearn could afford to be snippy.

'Thank you,' she said gratefully. 'I'll pay you for him, of course. How much do you want for him?'

'Nah.' The farmer reddened. 'She can have him free.' He grinned. 'Amy Haddon was my first girl-friend. She taught me "the Pride of Erin" and how to skim a stone to bounce five times before sinking. I reckon I owe her a favour. Now, how much of this here syrup do I feed the pup I'm keeping?'

Christy kept the pup in the back room for the rest of the day, with Ruth having strict instructions to pick it up and get as far from the pharmacy as she could if anyone the least official hove into view. Luckily the health inspectors kept their distance, and Christy locked the shop at five-thirty, picked up her warm little bundle of fluff and walked around to Amy's. Adam's car pulled up just as she arrived.

He had brought Amy home. As Christy approached, he took Amy's suitcase from the car boot and came around to help her from the car. Christy had expected her to have caught a taxi home earlier.

It was too late to turn back now. Both Adam and Amy had seen her. They stood and waited while she approached. Amy smiled a greeting, but Adam's face was still.

'Welcome home, Amy,' Christy said, struggling for words. 'I thought. . .' She resolutely faced Amy. 'I thought you'd be home earlier.'

'Dr McCormack said he'd drop me off home after his surgery,' Amy told her. 'Seeing as we're nearly neighbours now.' She glanced over to her left at Adam's cottage, a lawn width away.

'I'll bring a casserole around later,' Christy prom-ised, resolutely ignoring Adam. 'But this little one walked into my pharmacy this afternoon and told me it wanted a good home.' She held up her wriggling fluff ball. 'His name is Bounce and he tells me he's a great watch-dog.'

Amy's face went still. For an awful moment Christy thought she was going to cry. Oh, heck, she thought frantically. She's allergic to dogs. She hates dogs, I've done the wrong thing. . .

And then Amy was reaching out with the hand that wasn't encased in a sling, taking the wee pup into her arms. 'Oh, Christy. . .' She whispered. She looked down at the tiny pup and a tear slid down to land on the puppy's head. 'I've never had a dog,' she said softly. 'Bill wouldn't. . .'

'Well, you have one now,' Christy told her. 'If you want him.'

'Bounce. . .' Amy smiled down as the puppy wriggled. 'Why call him Bounce?'

'He's payment for five bounces.' Christy grinned. 'He comes from Matthew Hearn. You taught Matthew how to skim-bounce a stone five times. Bounce is to be considered payment in full.'

'But Edith Hearn. . .' Amy started, her voice faltering in disbelief.

'You're not to listen to town tattle,' Christy said roundly. 'There are many here who are fond of you, if you'll let us close.' She looked up to find Adam's eyes on her, and the expression in his eyes made her gasp. He had no business to look at her like that. Not unless. . . Flushing, she looked back at Amy. 'I'd better go now,' she said, and her voice wasn't quite steady. 'But my mum always told me that when I was in distress I should make no life decisions and I should only listen to people who like me. It's good advice.' She leaned over the wriggling Bounce and kissed Amy solidly on the cheek. 'I'll be back later with the casserole.'

'Christy, wait,' Adam said urgently.

She shook her head, already moving away.

'You go,' Amy told Adam, seeing his wish to speak to Christy. 'I can take my things inside.'

Adam cast a look at the fast retreating Christy and then turned back, shaking his head. 'It can wait,' he told Amy. 'The most important thing is to get you and this ball of fluff Miss Blair tells us is a dog settled back into your home. Besides,' he said as he picked up Amy's suitcase for the second time, 'I have a proposition to put to you.'

Christy walked on.

Two hours later she returned with the promised casserole. It was hard to make herself come back. Living two doors from Amy, Adam was too close for comfort. Still, she had promised the casserole. If she thought the town ladies would be looking after Amy she wouldn't have bothered, but she thought no such thing.

Amy welcomed her with a smile, and carefully locked the door after her.

'You needn't have bothered, dear,' she told Christy. 'You and Dr McCormack have done so much for me already.' She motioned to a sleeping fluff bundle in the corner. 'And now you've given me company. And Dr McCormack. . .' She gave a sudden gasp as though catching herself in mid-sentence and ended up lamely, 'Well, he's been so kind as well.'

'You were my friend when I first came to this town,' Christy told her, putting the casserole on the table. 'When I moved house you made me a casserole. The favour is now returned.'

'It's not returned now until I've given you a dog.' To Christy's delight Amy smiled broadly, a smile of contentment and happiness. Christy almost stared. She hadn't seen that smile. . . Well, she hadn't seen that smile in the two years she'd known Amy.

'I need a dog like I need a sore toe,' she said firmly. She looked down at her foot. 'And I can do without another sore toe.'

Amy chuckled and once again Christy stared. Something had happened to Amy. Was it just the pup?

'I hope Dr McCormack settled you in all right,' she said tentatively.

'Oh, yes.' Amy's smile slipped a little. 'He wanted to tell me about Tom.'

'Your son?'

'Yes.' Amy picked up the kettle. 'Tea?' Without waiting for an answer she put the kettle on to boil, using it as a reason to turn her back to Christy. 'He found Tom for me and told him Bill was dead. Tom already knew. It doesn't make any difference. Tom doesn't want anything to do with me.'

Christy was silent for a moment, hearing the break in Amy's voice. The laughter had gone. 'How does that make you feel?' she asked.

'Terrible.' Amy squared her shoulders and turned back to Christy. 'But no worse than I was feeling before. I think I've known it for a long time now. If Tom had been interested he would have contacted me before this.' She sighed. 'I should have walked out on Bill when Tom was a lad. Bill was a violent drunk. He hit me and he hit Tom. Things were different then, though. I never went past third form at school. I married young and I could no more earn my own living than fly. If I'd been on my own I might have left but there was Tom. I couldn't support him and Bill always said if I left he'd follow and take Tom from me.' She shrugged. 'I had nowhere to go.'

'So Tom blames you,' Christy said softly. 'Amy, it's so unfair.'

'Well, life's unfair,' Amy said stolidly. She sighed and then the smile crept back. 'But there's always something to look forward to.' She took a deep breath as though close to bursting with excitement. 'Dr McCormack has asked me to be his housekeeper.'

'His housekeeper,' Christy said blankly. She turned the idea over in her mind. 'That's an excellent idea,' she said slowly. 'Though with Dr McCormack's tiny cottage you'll find the work not exactly arduous.'

'You never know.' Amy carefully placed tea into the pot. Once again Christy was struck by her air of suppressed excitement. 'It might be more work than we think.' She smiled. 'It'll keep me busy for the next few days anyway. Dr McCormack's going away and he's asked me to do some work there while he's gone. Make it prettier.' She grinned happily. 'He's given me money to buy furniture. He's even paid Pete to take me over to Tynong on Monday in the taxi to choose what I need.'

Christy stared at her blankly. 'Going away. . .'

'Just for a few days,' Amy explained. 'He's going back to England.'

'Wh—why?' It was none of Christy's business but she couldn't stop the involuntary question. Amy didn't mind in the least.

'He says he has unfinished business,' she said primly. Her eyes twinkled. 'Oh, Christy. . .' She gasped again and put her lips firmly together. 'I mustn't say any more. But I have a job.' She bent over and scooped up her sleepy puppy and planted a kiss firmly on his small head. 'I have a job. I have a dog and I have two very good friends.' She smiled happily across at Christy. 'Who could ask for more?'

Christy left her half an hour later. She walked slowly across the lawn in the dark towards her car. Her mind was still numb with what she had learned.

It's none of my business what he's going to England for, she said to herself savagely. It's none of my business. Adam McCormack is nothing to me.

'Christy!'

She stopped as if struck. Adam was striding towards her through the shadows.

Christy stood stock-still waiting for him to reach her. Her mind wanted to get in the car fast and drive away but her legs wouldn't take her. This man is one of the Corrook doctors, she said to herself. I have a professional relationship with him. Nothing more.

'Have you a moment to talk?' Adam asked as he came to a halt before her.

'If you like,' she said cautiously, and then added ungraciously, 'What do you want?'

'The puppy was an inspiration,' he said, refusing to notice the edge of anger in her voice. His voice was calm and controlled, anything but the emotions Christy was feeling.

'Amy seems to like it.' She swallowed. 'She likes the idea of being your housekeeper too.' She bit her lip, unable to suppress the niggle of worry that had occurred to her when Amy told her of the job. 'Adam, you hardly need a housekeeper. You're never home. If Amy starts to think you've offered her the job from charity. . .'

'But I'm not,' he said calmly, stopping her in mid-sentence. 'I need a houskeeper.'

'You can even cook. . .'

He shrugged. 'I need a housekeeper,' he said firmly as though tired of the topic of conversation. 'Did Amy tell you I was going away?'

'Yes.' Christy made no comment. She stood, staring at the ground, miserably aware of Adam. He was so large, and so near. All she wanted was for him to touch her. To hold her. . .

But Adam was going to England.

'It's a flying visit,' he told her. 'I should be back next Wednesday.'

'It's no concern of mine when you come back,' she said tightly. 'Except that it's hardly fair on Richard and Kate.'

'I've talked to them, of course.' Adam was refusing to be drawn into her palpable anger. 'Kate's well enough now to give an anaesthetic if she has to. The hospital will look after the baby in an emergency. Richard will be worked into the ground but I can't help that. I have to go home.'

Home. . . The word hung over them like a cloud. Home is where the heart is, Christy thought miserably.

'Is there anything you wanted me for?' she asked dully. She turned to her car.

'You're not going to tell me to have a good trip?'

She shrugged. 'Have a good trip.'

'I will be back on Wednesday,' he said gently.

'It's nothing to me when you do come back,' she burst out. 'Stay there for all I care.'

'That would leave Richard in a mess.'

'Well, it would get me out of one.'

Adam moved then. He took her shoulders and turned her to face him. 'Christy, don't.'

She was crying blindly. He pulled her into the soft fabric of his shirt. She stayed rigid for a moment, and then suddenly the fight went out of her.

'You can't expect me to be calm and rational,' she sobbed. 'Adam, you can't make love to me and then move away as if nothing's happened. I'm not like that. It's all or nothing.'

'The happy ending,' Adam said grimly. He gave a humourless laugh. 'The knight in white armour and the happy ever after.' He tilted her chin. 'I know,' he said bitterly. 'It's what you deserve.'

'Well, why can't I have it?' She gulped back a sob. 'Adam, I've fallen in love. Like a fool I fell in love five years ago.'

'But I fell in love before that,' Adam said sadly. 'With Sarah. And that love has left me with ghosts. Five years ago I met you and the memory of that meeting stayed with me. I came to Australia to flee the ghosts and because I wanted to find you. I wanted to know whether the memory I had was a romantic nonsense.' He ran his hands down her slim hips, holding her close to him. 'Well, I found you, and I found that the attraction between us all those years ago wasn't just a figment of my imagination. But the ghosts came too, Christy. There are responsibilities in England I can't avoid. There are ghosts I can't shrug off even if I wanted to. What's become clear to me is that I can't ask you to share them.' He shrugged. 'I hadn't thought things through before I left England—what I'd do if you were still the Christy I remembered. The thought that you might love me. . .' He stopped mid-sentence and then shrugged again. When he resumed talking his voice was bitter. 'Well, I can't ask you to share my past.'

Christy put up her hand and touched his drawn face. 'Adam, let me try,' she said softly. 'I love you so much. . .'

'Christy, leave it.' He was suddenly pushing her away, his face tight with pain. 'You don't know what you'd be letting yourself in for. I'm not going to let you commit yourself to me while there are still ghosts.' He shook his head. 'You're young and you're free. You said yourself that you want to have fun.'

'And we couldn't?'

He shook his head. He took a step back. 'I don't think you would,' he said bluntly. 'Not when you know. . .' He paused. 'I'll be back on Wednesday,' he said and his voice was suddenly harsh and businesslike. 'I've asked Amy if she'll spend some time making my house attractive. Would you mind keeping an eye on her?'

'Your house attractive,' Christy said blankly. 'Why?'

'I don't like living in dumps,' Adam told her. 'I want it looking good but I don't want Amy overworking. Could you check on her?'

'I can do that.' She frowned. 'Why the rush?'

'I told you. I want to come home to a decent place to live.' He gave a mocking smile. 'My last landlady spoiled me.'

'I'll check on Amy.' Christy was far from understanding and all of a sudden she was tired. She wanted the strain to be over. She turned away. 'Have a good trip,' she said dully.

'Christy?' The harshness had suddenly faded from Adam's voice. He sounded unsure.

'Yes?' She paused and half turned.

'I. . .' He stopped. For a moment they stayed looking at each other in the moonlight. Then, suddenly, Christy was seized by the shoulders and kissed hard. His kiss was demanding and cruel, a kiss of anger, desire and frustration. She could feel all these things. She could taste his anger.

She didn't return the kiss. Somehow she made herself go limp, passively refusing to respond. He mustn't be able to do this to her. He had offered her nothing. No love. No promises. Nothing. He demanded everything.

And she couldn't give it. Not when he was boarding a plane tomorrow to return to England. Not when he wanted to be with his ghosts.

CHAPTER ELEVEN

TRUE to her promise, Christy called in at Adam's small cottage over the next few days, and each time found Amy hard at work.

'You should be careful,' Christy warned her on her last visit. It was Tuesday and Adam would be back the next day. 'You're only three days out of hospital.'

'If it weren't for this darned plaster on my arm I'd be fine,' Amy said happily. She was scrubbing the veranda with one hand, laughing at Bounce as he barked with each movement of the scrubbing brush. She sat back on her heels and wiped away a stray strand of hair. 'Truly, Christy, I haven't been so busy for years, or so happy. Do you want to see what I've done?'

'I guess so.'

The little house gleamed. The cottage had been sadly neglected but Amy had worked wonders.

'I've made new curtains all through,' she said proudly. 'At least I will have by tomorrow. I've only the spare room to go.'

'The spare room. . .'

'Dr McCormack said he wanted the spare room to be special,' Amy told her. She threw open a door. 'What do you think?'

Christy stared. The spare room was indeed special.

'The whole place was painted inside last week,' Amy explained, seeing Christy's surprise. She smiled. 'The landlord did the painting. There's some things I can't do with this arm. But I chose the bed and dresser, and the furnishings. Isn't it pretty?'

It was indeed. The room was furnished in the softest of blues. The bedstead and dresser were both blue with

147

white trim. A blue and white patchwork quilt covered the bed and pale pink rugs covered the worn carpet. It looked fresh, lovely and very feminine.

'The quilt is from my place,' Mrs Haddon told her proudly. 'I never use it and it's lovely to know it will be appreciated.'

'It's very. . . It's very feminine.'

Amy nodded efficiently. She ushered Christy out and closed the bedroom door firmly behind her. 'That's what he wanted,' she said as if Adam's pronouncements were law and not open to discussion. 'Now I'd best lock up here and get on home. I have curtains to sew tonight, and with only one good hand it takes me three times as long as normal.'

For a moment — for a crazy moment — Christy almost offered to help. She realised in time what she was doing and bit her tongue. Spending the evening sewing curtains for Adam McCormack's female guests was not her idea of fun.

She walked back over the lawn to where she had parked the car outside Amy's house. Amy walked with her.

'Are you sure you're OK?' she asked Amy as they reached the car. She looked down at the woman's flushed face.

Amy grimaced. 'I need to go inside and have a sit for a while. The curtains can wait until after tea.'

Christy frowned. She reached up and touched Amy's forehead. 'You feel a bit feverish.'

'I've been scrubbing.' Amy shrugged. 'I'm feeling the heat a bit,' she admitted. 'I've had a heat rash for the last couple of days.'

'A rash. . .'

'It's nothing,' Amy assured her. 'Honestly. . .'

'Well, take it easy tonight,' Christy said severely. 'Maybe you'd better see Richard tomorrow. The curtains can wait.'

Adam's guests can wait, she thought bitterly.

She spent the remainder of her evening at home doing bookwork and trying not to think of Adam. Where was he now? Was he already on the plane heading back to Australia?

The night was the summer's hottest so far. The heat added to Christy's inability to concentrate. She struggled with a line of figures that wouldn't balance. On the third try she gave up. Adam *must* be on the plane by now, she decided, her mind refusing to let go its niggle of worry. If he *was* coming home. . .

Adam would hardly go to the trouble of renovating the cottage if he hadn't believed he was coming back, she told herself crossly. Of course he had to come back.

But what of the ghosts? What ties to England still existed?

She was going crazy. She added the figures one last time and then threw her pen aside in disgust. Nothing was working. Crossing to the phone, she dialled Richard and Kate's number.

'Kate?'

'Is something wrong, Christy?' Kate's concern sounded through the telephone.

Christy collected herself. Her voice was revealing her unhappiness and it was stupid to pass that unhappiness on to Kate.

'No, Kate. There's nothing wrong. I'm sorry to have disturbed you. . .'

'The phone's been going non-stop all night. You're my twentieth caller. If you tell me you need an urgent house call for a sore throat I shall scream and drum my heels on the floor.'

'I won't do that,' Christy smiled. She hesitated. 'I was just. . . I was just wondering whether Adam had called. . .'

'Why should Adam call? He'll be back tomorrow.'

That was all Christy needed to know. She put the

phone down feeling foolish. Two minutes later it rang again. It was Amy Haddon.

'Are you still awake, Christy?' Amy's voice sounded fearful, piercing Christy's misery.

'What is it, Amy?'

'You know you thought I was running a temperature?' she asked. She gave a frightened gasp. 'Christy. . . Christy, I just passed out.'

Christy drew in her breath. 'Are you sitting down now?' she demanded.

'Yes — yes.'

'Don't move. I'll be there as soon as I can.'

Five minutes later she was banging fruitlessly on Amy's front door. The house was as tightly locked as a fortress. Amy had always been careful and the events of the past few weeks had made her more so. Swiftly Christy made her way through the darkened garden to the back door. She knocked again, and to her relief this time she gained a response.

'Christy?' The voice sounded weak and frightened but any response was better than nothing. 'Is that you?'

'Sure is,' Christy called out. 'How do I get in?'

'I can't stand up,' Amy called faintly. 'Every time I stand I feeel all queer and I reckon I'll pass out again.'

'There's no key hidden in the back garden?'

'No — no.'

Christy looked down at her toe and shook her head ruefully. This was no screen door she was tackling.

The bathroom window looked over the back porch. She picked up a pot plant, took a deep breath and lobbed it dead centre. Soil and plant went everywhere and the window stayed intact.

'Christy?' Mrs Haddon sounded frightened.

'Don't worry,' she called, bending to pick up a heavier projectile. 'I just failed elementary burglary. You're down one pot of petunias. Next on the list is a garden gnome.'

'Not my Ernie. . .' The fear had made way for another anxiety.

'Ernie?'

'He's the gnome in the red hat.'

Christy reluctantly laid Ernie down. She picked up another gnome with spotted headgear. 'Spots OK?' she called.

'The spotty one's new. I don't like it much.' Amy was making an effort but the fear was back and there was a distinct tremor in her voice. Christy pulled her arm back and lobbed as hard as she could. The window splintered into a thousand pieces, the unfortunate gnome flew on and the mirror on the bathroom wall went the same way as the window.

'Talk about overkill,' Christy muttered. She grabbed the back-door mat and used it to shove the rest of the glass from the frame, then laid it over the sill. A minute later she was by Amy's side.

Where Amy three hours before had been flushed and ruddy in the face she was now white-faced. She was clinging to the arms of her chair as if she needed their support. She did. As she saw Christy she held out her hands and then swayed in her chair. She closed her eyes and gripped tighter.

'I'm so sorry,' she muttered. 'I've caused so much bother.'

'Don't be sorry,' Christy said gently. She gripped Amy's shoulders. 'Let's get you to bed, shall we?'

'I don't know what's wrong. . . I don't. . .' Amy shook her head weakly, tears of distress running down her face.

'You're running a fever,' Christy told her. She could feel it through the thin cotton of Amy's blouse. The woman was burning hot. The temperature in the house was hot but Amy was hotter. Christy bit her lip as she helped her through into the bedroom. Was there infection in the arm or in Amy's head wound? Something had to be behind this fever.

'I'll ring Richard—Dr Blair,' she told Amy as she helped her on to the bed.

'I don't. . . I don't want to be a bother.'

'I know you don't, Christy reassured her. 'You can't help being ill, though, and Dr Blair would be annoyed if I didn't ring him.' She wrenched up the bedroom window to try and get what little breeze there was circulating into the house and then went to telephone her brother.

She couldn't find him.

'Richard's still out on a call,' Kate told her. 'He went up to a farm at the head of the valley. What's wrong?'

She listened as Christy outlined what was happening. 'Maybe it's just a cold,' Christy told her. 'But I don't think so.'

'The antibiotics she had in hospital should still be doing their job,' Kate frowned. 'An infection would hardly be starting now. Unless. . .unless there's an abscess. . .'

'She's ill, Kate. This isn't just a cold in the head.'

'Have you a thermometer?'

'I'll see if Amy owns one.'

Three minutes later Christy was staring at the thin glass tube in concern. She crossed back to the telephone. 'Forty-one,' she told Kate. 'And Kate. . . I think she's getting delirious.'

'She'll have to come into hospital,' Kate said decisively. 'I'll ring the ambulance.'

Christy glanced worriedly through the bedroom door. Amy was tossing fretfully on the bed. 'Will you meet us there?'

'I'll see if I can contact Richard.' Kate hesitated. 'I've only just got Andrew to sleep. If Richard can't be at the hospital when the ambulance arrives I'll come, though. Keep her cool, Christy.'

Keep her cool. . . In this heat. . .

Christy's mind went over the advice she gave to mothers of children with mild fevers. Cool bath, leave

the clothes off and put on the fan. A bath was out of
the quesition but Christy could use a sponge. She filled
a bowl with cold water, found a fan and went back into
the bedroom. From then until the ambulance arrived
she concentrated on getting Amy's overheated body as
cool as she could.

Amy was slipping away from her in her mind.
Christy's efforts didn't seem to be working and as the
fever mounted so did Amy's distress. She tossed on the
bed, muttering unintelligibly. At one stage she
wrenched her injured arm and cried out in pain. Christy
swore in helplessness. There seemed nothing she could
do.

Then she heard the sound she had been waiting for —
a vehicle approaching fast. The ambulance wasn't using
its siren but its flashing light shone an eerie blue and
red glow through the bedroom window. Christy laid
down her sponge, cast a dubious look at the woman on
the bed and ran to open the front door.

She didn't wait for the men to come in. By now she
was fearful that Amy could really hurt herself as she
threw herself around the bed. She opened the door,
saw the ambulance pull up on the verge and then ran
back into the house. A minute later two ambulance
officers walked into the room. Behind them strode
Adam.

Adam. . . Christy stared as though not believing her
eyes. Under her hands Amy stirred and moaned and
then thrashed sideways on the bed. Christy turned back
to hold her still but not before she realised that four
people had come into the room. In his arms Adam
carried a child.

'What the hell's going on?' He was the first to speak.
The two ambulance officers turned to him, but he
motioned them aside impatiently. He placed the child
down in the depths of an armchair by the door. The
little girl looked up fearfully. 'Stay there, Fiona,' he

said firmly. He touched her lightly and left her, striding swiftly to the bed. 'Now, tell me. . .'

Christy had no more thoughts to spare for the tiny, waif-like child near the door. Not yet. Adam placed a hand on Amy's wrist and withdrew it as if it burnt him.

'Is there a bath here?' he snapped.

'Yes.' Christy nodded. She'd checked the bathroom in her search for a thermometer.

'Fill it,' he ordered one of the ambulance officers. 'It's so hot we're not going to get her cool any other way. Put enough hot water in it to take the worst of the chill from it but leave it cold. Fast!' The man was already moving.

'Let's move her in there,' Adam told the other officer. 'If we don't get that temperature down she's going to convulse.'

'Do we strip her, Doc?' the ambulance officer said dubiously.

'No.' Adam was already pulling Amy's sensible work shoes from her feet. 'Leave her dress on. Wet clothes will help keep her cool until we get her into the hospital's air-conditioning. Christy, how long has she been like this?'

'She was fine three hours ago,' Christy told him. 'I don't understand. Would an infection work this fast?'

'I don't think this is wound infection.' The ambulance officers had brought in a stretcher. While he talked Adam was helping the ambulanceman lift Amy across to the canvas. 'If there's an abscess brewing in her head, though. . . Hold her steady while we move her into the bathroom, Christy. I don't want her to roll off.' He cast a anxious glance at the huddled child on the chair and then deliberately looked away. The child looked confused, frightened and totally bereft but Amy needed all his attention. 'Lift,' he ordered. 'Help us in with her, Christy, and then ring the hospital. If Intensive Care's not in use I want it prepared before we get there, with the temperature as low as they can manage.'

By the time Christy had made the phone call, Adam's unorthodox treatment was taking effect. Amy's delirium was fading. She lay back in the bath, disorientated and embarrassed. As Christy reported back to Adam, she started to protest but Adam held her there. 'A little longer, Mrs Haddon. We'll just make sure you stay nice and cold until we get you to hospital.'

'But what's wrong with me?' Amy wailed weakly. 'Oh, Dr McCormack. . .' Then, as she realised whom she was talking to, she said in bewilderment, Dr McCormack. You're home,' she whispered. 'I haven't made the curtains yet.' And then, as the mists cleared still further, she frowned. 'Did you bring the wee one back with you. . .?' Her voice trailed off in confusion.

'I did,' Adam told her. 'Now relax and don't worry.' He smiled at Amy in the way that Christy knew would make that lady do whatever this man asked of her. 'Christy,' he said slowly, without turning. 'Could you check Fiona, please?'

The little girl. . . She would still be huddled in the bedroom. Christy gave a gasp of concern and whisked out of the bathroom. She didn't have a clue what was going on but the look of the child was enough to wrench at her heart.

The child hadn't moved. She hadn't made a sound. She was staring straight ahead at a point above the bed. When Christy bent to touch her she didn't respond at all.

She must be about four, Christy guessed. She was a tiny, elfin-like creature with thin brown hair pulled severely into braids and huge green eyes all but enveloping her face. Christy knelt and took two stiff little hands into hers.

'I'm Christy,' she said. She took a deep breath as things fell into place. Those eyes were unmistakable.

'Your daddy asked me to look after you while he's busy.'

For a long moment she thought the child hadn't heard her. The fixed gaze didn't waver. The hands stayed rigid in her clasp. And then, slowly, the big green eyes filled with tears and the child's body shuddered in one long sob. Christy's heart wrenched within her. She scooped the child to her and held her hard.

The sobbing went on and on. It wasn't noisy. If Christy hadn't felt the shudders running through the little girl's body she wouldn't even have known it was happening. She could feel them only too clearly, though. She sat and crooned and rocked and crooned and rocked, her hand stroking the ridiculous tight braids, waiting until the child's fear, loneliness and distrust cried itself out.

From the outer room came sounds of Amy being lifted from the bath. A minute later Adam appeared at the bedroom door. His face was tight with worry.

'Is Richard at the hospital, Christy?'

'No.' In Christy's arms the little girl was almost asleep. She stirred at the sound of Adam's voice but Christy's arms tightened. It was cruel but the child was going to have to make do with her for a while longer. 'He's out on a call. Kate says she'll come if she has to.'

'I might need her. I don't know what the hell is going on.' Adam looked helplessly down at the little girl. 'I was bringing Fiona home and the ambulance pulled up just in front of me. I could hardly. . .'

'You had to come,' Christy said gently, understanding his anguish. 'Adam, I'll take Fiona over to your house and wait for you there.'

'No.' He shook his head. 'A walk in the dark and yet another house. . .' He bent and touched the sleepy little girl on the face. 'This is Christy, Fiona. Christy is my friend. Fiona, do you remember me telling you I look after sick people?'

'You're a doctor,' Fiona said flatly. Her voice was
sleep-laden and still tear-filled.

'That's right. Fiona, I have to look after a sick lady
now. The lady you saw just now. I'll take her to the
hospital and when I. . .when I've made her better I'll
come back and take you to your new home. Until then
Christy will look after you. Is that OK?'

'OK,' the child said tearfully in a voice that made it
quite clear that it wasn't OK at all. Adam sighed. He
looked haggard.

'Go on,' Christy said gently. 'Fiona and I will sleep.'

Christy didn't move for a long time after Adam left.
She couldn't. Fiona was sleeping, but only just. Every
now and then her body would give a convulsive shudder
as though remembering the terrors around her.

What on earth was Adam doing with the child? This
was crazy. Where had the child been until now? Christy
fingered the little girl's braids, her hands itching to
undo them. They were so tightly braided, they looked
as if they hurt. The child was dressed in a severe grey
skirt and travel-stained white blouse. Her braids were
held in place with elastic bands and nothing else.

Had she been in some sort of institution? That was
what she looked like. Christy shook her head, a slow
anger building inside her. What was Adam McCormack
playing at, to leave this child in England when he came
here? Was this the ghost he was trying to escape from?
Christy's vision of another woman back in England
faded, but her anger was greater than anything she
would have felt if Adam had appeared with a fiancée
in tow. He had said the ghosts couldn't be escaped.
How could he have possibly wanted to try and escape
this little one?

Christy found she was crying, hugging the little girl
to her, singing meaningless little children's rhymes that
came from nowhere. . .rhymes her mother had sung to
her but had been forgotten long since. Now they

surfaced to be used again, for a little girl who needed them so much more.

Finally the child's body relaxed. At last her sleep became deep and relaxed. Christy's knees were stiffening where she sat. Carefully she lifted the little girl over on to the bed and drew the sheet up to her face. The child whimpered once and then settled.

For a long moment Christy stood staring down at the tear-stained little face. She had never seen a child so defenceless. Her anger built into a tight knot of rage. She had thought she loved Adam McCormack. How could she love a man who had treated a child like this?

She left the light on in the bedroom while she went into the kitchen. She'd make some tea, she thought. A hot drink might calm her a little. The night had held too much for her tired mind to cope with.

What on earth was happening with Amy? Was there an abscess forming in the cavity where the brain had bled? Christy thought through all the possibilities she could think of and discarded them one after the other. One she liked. A urinary tract infection, she told herself. It could just be that. That and too much physical work on a hot day. . .

She picked up the telephone and dialled the hospital. The night sister answered on the second ring.

'Dr Blair's still out of the valley,' the sister told her. 'Thank heaven Dr McCormack's here. No, we don't know what's wrong yet. Dr McCormack has done a chest X-ray and eliminated possiblities such as a UTI. Now he's thinking we might have to transfer her to Melbourne tonight. She needs a CAT scan.'

He still suspected an abscess. Christy put the phone down with a heavy heart. The prognosis in such an eventuality was grim. The kettle boiled. She checked that Fiona was still sleeping soundly and then sat down at the kitchen bench with a mug of hot, sweet tea. On the second sip a small bottle of medication caught her eye.

If it had been a bottle from her own pharmacy Christy would not have picked it up, but she was curious. Amy had sworn she had got rid of all the Valium and scripts she had ever had, and anything else should have come through Blair Pharmacy. Maybe this was medication the Melbourne hospital had given her while she was there. Christy picked up the bottle and turned the label towards her. Frowning, she tipped the pills out on to the bench and counted. Then she reached for the phone.

'I want to speak to Dr McCormack,' she told the startled night sister.

'He can't come, Miss Blair,' the sister told her. 'Mrs Haddon is really very sick. . .'

'I know,' Christy snapped. 'That's why I want to talk to him. Now get him, fast!'

A minute later Adam was on the phone. He sounded at the end of his tether.

'I hope this is important, Christy. . .'

'Adam, Amy's been taking blood-pressure pills,' she said abruptly. She turned the label to her and read its information to him.

'So?' Adam could clearly see no need for the information Christy was supplying. 'Christy, I have to go. Is Fiona —— ?'

Christy sighed and broke in again. 'Fiona's fine. Adam, I know you're busy but you must listen to me. The date on the bottle says Amy received these pills six months ago, but there are only a few pills missing. Two days' dosage in fact. The bottle's on the kitchen bench as though she's taking them now. If Amy started taking these two days ago for the first time. . .'

'I can't see. . .'

'Adam, these pills have a rare but documented side-effect. Fever.'

Silence.

Then, 'Are you sure?' he asked cautiously, and Christy could tell from his voice that he was examining the idea from all sides and matching it with the symptoms he was treating.

'I'm sure. I usually warn doctors who prescribe it to be careful, but this prescription hasn't been issued through my pharmacy. Mild fever with a rash is an uncommon reaction to the drug, but there have been reported instances of excessive fever. Not many, but enough to be reported.'

'You obviously keep up with your literature.' Adam was obviously thinking fast. 'If that's all that's causing this. . .'

Christy took a deep breath. 'I couldn't assume it, Adam, but we could hope. If it is, then in twenty-four hours the stuff should have worked out of her system. . .' She hesitated. 'Is she rational now?'

'Yes.'

'Ask her if she's taken the drug before,' Christy told him. 'The timing is right and the symptoms are spot-on.'

'She hasn't had any headaches,' he said slowly. He was no longer talking to her. He was talking to himself. 'Nothing that's suggestive of abscess. . .' There was a moment's silence, then a curt, 'Thanks, Christy,' and the phone was put down.

The worry hanging over Christy had lightened a little. She might be wrong, but the thought of the alternative was horrendous. Buoyed, she went out to the bathroom and inspected the damage her gnome had inflicted. The backboard of the smashed mirror fitted easily over the broken window-frame. She found nails and a hammer in the laundry, stepping over the soundly sleeping Bounce as she searched, and nailed the broken window shut.

She checked on Fiona again but, like the puppy, the child was deeply asleep. There was nothing more for Christy to do but sit and wait.

An hour later Adam woke her. She was asleep at the

kitchen bench, her head cradled on her arms. She woke as he touched her lightly on the shoulder.

'A-Adam. . .' For a moment she was confused, and then the events of the night flooded back. She shook the last vestige of sleep from her head and rose stiffly to her feet. 'How—how's Amy?'

'We've sent her to Melbourne,' he told her, then at her look of dismay he shook his head. 'No, we're not sure it's an abscess. I'm hoping like hell that your idea is the right one, but Richard and I discussed it and decided we couldn't take the risk of keeping her. If she has intercranial bleeding and we miss it. . .' He shrugged. 'Hopefully the CAT scan will show nothing.' He sank down on to the stool Christy had vacated and put his head in his hands. 'She's sleeping normally, though, and we think we have her temperature under control. If you're right, then she should be recovering by morning.'

'It was the first time she'd taken the pills?' Christy asked. Adam looked like a man who had gone past the point of total exhaustion. He looked grey. She turned on the kettle and made another mug of strong, sweet tea. She handed it to him and he took it as if he were being handed a lifeline.

'Thanks, Christy. I don't know. . .' He shook his head as though he had lost the thread of conversation. 'Yes, it was the first time she'd taken them. A doctor a few months ago—one of the city doctors she visited to get Valium—told her she had high blood-pressure and included the script for the blood-pressure pills with the Valium. She had to get the blood-pressure pills to get the Valium but she decided not to take them. At that stage she was so depressed that the thought of an early death through high blood-pressure seemed even appealing. Then, this week, she suddenly decided she had something to live for, so without consulting anyone she took the damned things.'

'But she's OK now?'

'If you're right. . . As long as we can keep the temperature down she'll be OK and the ambulance is air-conditioned. Richard's gone with her.'

'I'm glad.'

There was silence as Adam finished his tea. Christy stood and watched. It was surreal. The events of the night weren't really happening. There was no waif-like child in the next room. This man couldn't possibly be Fiona's father. She gave herself a mental shake as Adam put down his coffee-mug.

'Take Fiona home now,' Christy told him. He was looking as dazed as she felt. In four days he had been to London and back and gained a daughter. 'I'll lock up here and I'll take Amy's puppy home with me.'

'Christy. . .'

'Go on,' she told him. 'Your daughter needs you and you both need bed. Pick up your daughter and go.' Try as she might she couldn't stop the raw edges of pain sounding in her voice. Adam looked uncertainly up at her.

'You're right, Christy,' he said quietly. 'I'll phone you tomorrow.'

She shook her head. 'I don't think that would be a good idea,' she said.

CHAPTER TWELVE

ADAM and his daughter came into the pharmacy the next afternoon. Somehow Christy had managed to get herself to work, although she wasn't sure how. Wednesday was market day and the town was busy. It was especially busy in Christy's pharmacy. Word of events of the night before swept through the town seemingly before breakfast and she had been grilled five times before she even got to work.

And is it true that Dr McCormack has asked Mrs Haddon to take care of his daughter during the day?' the fiftieth town matron into Blair Pharmacy for the day sniffed.

'I believe so,' Christy murmured, tired of the inquisitions.

'Hmph!' the lady muttered. 'He must trust her, then.'

'He has no reason not to,' Christy said gently.

'Hmph!' the lady said again but this time a little less decisively. She fingered a row of elastic bandages as if wondering whether to buy one. 'Amy Haddon's still in Melbourne, isn't she?' she asked.

'She will be until tomorrow,' Christy told her, her smile revealing the relief she was feeling at the news Richard had brought back. 'She's much better, though.'

'I'll visit her when she gets back,' the woman said decisively. 'There's been some nasty talk around this town about Amy Haddon, and I for one am very glad to be able to say I never believed it for a moment.'

Christy suppressed a smile. It seemed Amy would receive a lot of visitors before she escaped from hospital, and Christy rather doubted that she would be

163

needed to make a casserole when Amy came home. Amy Haddon had suddenly become a desirable and interesting person to know. She looked up and the inclination to smile died within her as Adam and his little girl entered the shop.

'Hello,' she said softly, addressing herself to Fiona. For answer Fiona stuck her finger in her mouth and moved closer to her father.

'Do you remember Christy from last night?' Adam asked. He picked the little girl up in his arms and turned to Christy. 'Miss Blair is a very clever pharmacist, Fiona.' He smiled. 'Fiona and I would like to thank you for looking after her last night.'

It was absurdly formal. Christy looked at the pair of them. Adam still looked as if he needed two days' sleep, and Fiona. . .well, Fiona was still dressed in those awful clothes. Her hair had been braided again, not as tightly this time but not expertly either. One braid started above her ear and the other almost below.

Christy moved across to touch the little girl lightly on the hair. 'It was a pleasure,' she said. Fiona buried her face deeply into her father's shoulder.

'Fiona?'

There was no verbal response. One green eye peered up from the safety of her father's shirt. Fiona looked at Christy as though she was afraid Christy might bite.

'Fiona, I have a rack of beautiful hair ribbons over here,' Christy told her. 'As a welcome to Australia, I'd like you to choose a pair.'

The eye subsided and was lost from view.

Christy turned to her assistant and smiled. 'Ruth, do we still have the red hair ribbons with little grey koalas all over them?' she asked.

'Sure we do,' Ruth smiled, summing up the situation with accuracy. 'There's only one pair left, though, Miss Blair.' She grinned happily. 'If someone was to want them I reckon they'd better move fast. They're the most popular hair ribbons in town.'

Two eyes emerged. Two eyes fixed Christy in a determined stare. 'Is it. . .a present?' she asked.

'Definitely a present,' Christy assured her. She crossed to the display stand and picked up the ribbons. Another customer walked into the shop and Ruth moved reluctantly away to serve him. Christy held out the hair ribbons. 'What do you think, Fiona?'

There was a long silence while Fiona considered. Christy glanced up at Adam. He was as intent as his daughter, as though she was making a decision of immense importance for them both. Finally Fiona pulled a small hand out from where it was tucked against Adam's chest and took the ribbons. 'Thank you very much,' she whispered. She looked at Christy. 'Are they really mine to keep?'

'Absolutely,' Christy promised. 'Would you like me to put them in your hair for you?'

'No, thank you,' she said, with touching formality.

Christy nodded as though she had expected nothing less. Then she had an inspiration. At the front of the shop was a rack of stuffed toys. Christy walked swiftly across and from the back of the pile she retrieved a small, stuffed koala. 'It's your lucky day, Fiona,' she smiled at the little girl. 'It just so happens that with every pair of koala hair ribbons sold in the store today the customer receives free one Kimberley Koala.' She snuggled the stuffed toy into the little girl's hands and the child's face lit with delight.

She didn't say a word. She stared at the toy koala, then back to Christy and then back to the koala. Finally, as if it was all too much, she buried her face in her father's shoulder again. Kimberley Koala was buried deep in the folds of Adam's shirt. She was, Christy gathered, acceptable. She smiled up at Adam and then her smile died on her lips. His face was raw with pain. He was staring at her as if he was seeing one of his ghosts.

'Christy ——' he started.

'Miss Blair. . .' Ruth interrupted from the other side of the shop. 'I'm sorry to interrupt but I need some advice here.'

Christy looked up at Adam and nodded dismissively, her face bleak. There was nothing he could say that she wanted to hear.

'I'm coming,' she told Ruth. She touched Fiona lightly on the shoulder. 'Enjoy your hair ribbons,' she told her, and then added a shaft. 'Tell your daddy to buy you a dress to match.'

Adam didn't rise to the implied criticism. 'That's what we're about to do,' he said evenly. 'Tell us where to go, Miss Blair.' He looked straight at her, the pain still behind his eyes. 'Which shop sells children's clothes?'

'There's no choice,' she told him. 'Nan's Frocks have some.'

'That's where we'll go, then.' He lifted Fiona from his shoulder so that he could see her face. 'Ok, Fi?'

The child didn't respond. She clutched her hair ribbons in one hand, her koala in the other and waited until he lowered her once more to his shoulder. Christy once more saw pain cross his face.

'Thank you,' he said formally. Christy stood watching until man and child disappeared from view. They both seemed bereft.

'Miss Blair. . .' Ruth's voice cut into her preoccupation. Reluctantly she turned.

'Yes, Ruth,' she said mechanically, her mind still on the pair who had just left.

'Miss Blair, could you give Mr Farquharson some advice, please? He would like some indigestion tablets.'

Christy frowned in irritation. Ruth knew where the antacid was kept. Then she caught herself, remembering the doctrine she had instilled over and over again into her assistant. 'Think about what the customer is saying and if there is the slightest — and I mean the *slightest*—doubt in your mind about what they want and the reasons they want it then refer them to me.' Because she was preoccupied there was no reason for Ruth to ignore the rule, and there would be a reason why the girl had referred to her. Christy crossed to the other side of the shop and summoned a smile for the elderly man beside Ruth.

'How may we help you, Mr Farquharson?'

'I just want some tablets for me heartburn,' the elderly farmer told her, annoyed. His speech was slightly breathless as if he was having trouble getting enough air. 'Simple enough. I dunno why the girl here can't get me some.'

'Sure.' Christy defused the farmer's annoyance by picking up a packet of antacid tablets. 'These are pretty mild, Mr Farquharson. I can give you stronger. How bad's the heartburn?'

'Bloody terrible,' the farmer said bluntly. 'If you've got stronger, then give me stronger.'

'You haven't suffered much from indigestion in the past,' Ruth interjected.

The farmer flashed her a look of annoyance. 'How the hell do you know that, girl?'

Ruth blushed crimson and stared at the floor. 'I. . . well, I haven't sold you indigestion tablets before. Or Mrs Farquharson either for that matter. And you sound terrible, Mr Farquharson.' She looked miserably over at Christy, aware that she was handling the crusty old man badly. 'The Farquharsons are our neighbours,' she explained.

Christy nodded, seeing clearly why she had been summoned. While the farmer was talking she had been watching him. He was breathless and sweating profusely. It was a hot day, but he looked. . .he looked as if he was in trouble.

'Could you organise the banking, Ruth?' Christy asked her gently, giving her a chance to leave. The farmer was clearly going to admit nothing in front of his next-door neighbour's child. 'I'll get you the stronger antacid, Mr Farquharson. Tell me where the pain is.'

The man cast a triumphant glance at the unfortunate Ruth and turned back to Christy. 'That's more like it. A man knows what's wrong with him.' He caught his breath suddenly, his right hand rose involuntarily towards his left shoulder and then he let it fall.

'Are you having sharp pain?' Christy asked.

'No,' he told her. 'Sharp pain could be my heart, couldn't it? This is real indigestion. It's like a tight band pulling tighter. Bloody thing. Dunno what I ate. . .'

'And the pain's going into your left arm?' she said quietly, watching the way he held it.

'A bit,' he admitted.

Christy nodded, wondering how to handle things from here on. She lifted a bottle of antacid mixture from the shelf, her mind racing.

'Would you like a dose before you leave?' she asked.

The farmer sighed. 'I would and all, Miss Blair, and that's a fact.' He looked over to make sure Ruth was out of earshot. 'I don't mind admitting to you that it's terrible bad.'

Christy took a deep breath. 'Mr Farquharson, I would like you to see a doctor,' she said firmly. 'I'd like to be sure the pain you're describing is not heart pain.'

The farmer snorted. He reached over and grabbed the bottle from her grasp. Thrusting his hand in his pocket, he drew out a large denomination note and shoved it on the counter.

'You can keep your medical opinions to yourself,' he said savagely, his bitterness slightly marred by breathlessness. 'Bloody women. First my wife and then my daughter and now you lot. Fuss! All over a bit of indigestion. Give me my change and let me get out of here.'

Christy nodded, her eyes on the man before her. She knew the sound of fear when she heard it and it was in the elderly farmer's voice loud and clear. 'Will you at least let us call. . .?'

She got no further. The effort to raise his voice had cost the farmer dear. His eyes widened as if in shock. He lifted his hands to clutch his chest and then slowly, agonisingly slowly, crumpled forward. Christy caught him before he hit the floor.

'Ruth!' she called urgently but the girl was already there. She had been watching in concern. Now she helped take the farmer's weight from Christy and they lowered him down.

'He's. . .' Ruth stared down in horror at the man at her feet. 'Oh, miss. . . He's dead. . .'

'Not yet, he's not,' Christy muttered savagely. She shoved her hand on the farmer's neck, searching desperately for a pulse. There wasn't one. She gave up the search, grabbed the buttons of the farmer's shirt and ripped. Buttons flew in either direction but Christy was already placing her hands over the farmer's chest and thumping down with all her might. What had she been told? If it's not hard enough to break ribs then it's not hard enough.

'I'll ring the ambulance. . .' Ruth was already running towards the telephone.

'No.' Christy thumped down hard again. 'Adam. . . Dr McCormack. He'll be two doors up in Nan's Frocks. Run, Ruth. Find him and then ring the ambulance.' She leaned forward and breathed her patient. His chest rose with the breath and the thumping began again. 'Run.' She was talking to thin air. Ruth had already gone.

The time Adam took seemed forever but in reality it must have been less than two minutes. He came into the shop at a run — and stopped short. Behind him came Ruth. She didn't stop but ran straight for the phone. Before she reached it Adam was kneeling beside the farmer.

'Keep breathing, Christy,' he ordered. 'You're doing fine. I'll do CPR.' In one swift movement they had changed places, he kneeling over the farmer's chest to give maximum thrust downwards and Christy at the farmer's head.

They worked together in rhythm. Christy counted strokes and breathed. Please. . .she was saying to herself. Please. . .

Seven, eight, nine. . . Christy leaned to breathe again and Adam caught her. 'No,' he said. 'This time wait.'

'Nothing.'

One, two, three. . .

And then it happened. The farmer's mouth moved fractionally and his breath was drawn in on a rasping, pain-filled breath that seemed as if it would tear him apart. Adam's fingers unclenched from the farmer's chest. The chest rose and fell of its own accord.

'Oh, God,' Christy murmured. 'Oh, thank God. . .'

There was the sound of a siren and suddenly Christy was redundant. She stood back while Adam and the ambulance officers took over. A cluster of people were milling around the door. Christy looked up through shocked eyes. They were blocking the stretcher's path. Adam was moving swiftly beside the stretcher, impatiently pushing a path. Christy understood the rush. At the hospital was the electrical defibrillator. . . everything they needed if he arrested again. They had to hurry.

And then, as they climbed into the ambulance, Adam cast a frantic look around and caught her eye over the heads of the gathering crowd.

'Christy, Fiona. . .' He called. The ambulance doors swung shut behind him. The siren wailed and the ambulance was gone.

'Fiona. . .' Christy turned to Ruth in horror. 'Where did he leave Fiona?'

Ruth put her hand to her mouth. 'Oh, miss. I forgot the little one. I guess she'll still be at Nan's Frock's.'

'Put a sign up saying closed, will you, Ruth?' Christy said savagely. 'Men! Of all the. . .'

'What was he supposed to do?' Ruth said reasonably. 'You couldn't have expected him to take her home before he attended Mr Farquharson.' Ruth was white-faced herself, and her voice wasn't quite steady.

'No — no,' Christy said quietly. 'But to do what he's done to that child. . .' She collected herself as she realised that Ruth was shaking. 'I'm sorry,' she said ruefully. 'Put up the sign, Ruth. Except for urgent scripts, Blair Pharmacy is closed.' She turned and walked from the shop.

Fiona was still in Nan's Frocks. Nan looked up gratefully as Christy appeared. 'Oh, Christy, love,' she said tearfully. 'What a dreadful thing. . . Is he OK?'

'I don't know,' Christy said shortly. 'Fiona. . .'

'She's in the changing-room. We had her in there changing when Ruth came for Dr McCormack. She hasn't moved since. She won't talk to me. I tried to pick her up and give her a cuddle but every time I go near her she backs into the corner as if I'm the big, bad wolf.'

Christy nodded. How on earth could a four-year-old cope with this? She slipped off her white coat and stepped through into the changing-room.

'Fiona?'

The child was absolutely still. Her eyes were huge in her white face. She was as Christy had seen her the night before, bereft and absolutely alone. Christy reached out for the little girl but she shrank from her outstretched hands. Christy sighed and sat down on the floor. Ignoring the child's shrinking, she pulled herself against the wall so that they were seated side by side.

'It was another patient,' she said conversationally.

'This one had a heart attack. Your daddy had to work really hard to make him better.'

There was no response at all.

'I guess this seems pretty scary,' she went on. 'Your daddy keeps leaving you in strange places when sick people need him. But it's not really strange, you know. We're your friends.'

Silence.

'And you have Kimberley,' Christy said reasonably. She reached out and touched the tiny stuffed toy. Fiona suffered her to touch it for a split-second and then the koala was withdrawn. 'Everyone needs a friend when their dad has to leave them for a little while,' Christy continued. 'I guess Kimberley's yours. Do you have any other friends?'

'No.' It was a scared whisper.

Christy nodded. 'Then I'm glad Kimberley's found you,' she said firmly. 'Kimberley didn't have any friends either. She's been looking for a special friend for ages. She's sat on the top shelf of my shop and inspected everyone who's come in. You were the very first person she wanted to go to.'

Fiona inspected the koala critically. 'Really?' she said, trying not to sound pleased.

'Cross my heart,' Christy promised.

'How do you know Kimberley's a girl?'

'How do I know. . .? Your daddy told me, of course,' Christy told her. 'Your daddy knows these things. He's a doctor.'

'How does he know?'

Christy grinned. 'Beats me,' she admitted. 'Why don't you ask him?'

'Will he come back?'

'Sure he'll be back,' Christy said solidly. 'Have you done enough clothes shopping?'

'I don't think I want clothes,' Fiona said sadly.

'We'll worry about them another time.' Christy rose and held out her hand. 'I think you should wait for

Daddy back in my shop. I have another friend hidden in my back room who you'd just love to meet. His name is Bounce.'

By the time Adam returned, his daughter was fast asleep. Christy had brought a couple of big towels into the pharmacy that morning for Bounce to sleep on. Fiona had settled on them to wait. With Bounce and Kimberley Koala she seemed almost content.

Wisely Christy let her be. She made her presence felt as she moved around the shop restocking shelves or making up urgent prescriptions but she didn't intrude. Christy was an adult, and Fiona didn't seem to have a lot of faith in adults. Who could blame her? Christy thought grimly. When Fiona drifted into sleep, puppy nestled on one side and koala tucked tight on the other side Christy gave a silent sigh of relief. Fiona's bed was none too hygienic but it was the best place for her.

Her anger was building as each moment passed. She was like a time bomb, with the detonation point already past. Each time she went to check on the sleeping child her anger built. How could Adam do this?

He walked in while she was out the back, striding through the empty shop to find them. She was bending over the sleeping child, shifting the sleepy puppy back from Fiona's face. Adam laid a hand on her shoulder and she jumped a foot.

'Christy?'

She motioned for him to be quiet. She rose and walked through to the main section of the pharmacy. Adam stood looking at his sleeping daughter for a moment and then followed her out.

'How is he?' she said tightly, as he entered the pharmacy.

'Still alive.' He sounded drained and flat. 'And lucky to be that. Thanks to you. . .'

'You did it. I didn't have the strength.'

Silence. Adam nodded. 'Thank you for looking after Fiona again,' he said quietly. 'I'll take her home now.'

'Can you guarantee you won't be called again?' The edge of anger in Christy's voice was unmistakable.

'Mr Farquharson seems to be stable. Richard's at the hospital. As long as there's no emergency. . .'

'And if there is?' Her voice was icy and her blue eyes flashed fire. 'What if there is, Adam McCormack? What are you going to do then? Abandon her again?'

'Christy, I couldn't help this. I'd organised Amy Haddon to take care of her while I was working. I didn't count on. . .'

'Who did you organise to look after her when you abandoned her in England?' she snapped. 'What happened to her then? Was that some paid employee too? What sort of a rotten father are you to treat a little girl like that?' Her anger was white-hot and she was past caring about what she said. The vision of Fiona huddled at the back of Nan's changing-room was burned into her mind and she didn't have to go past it to fuel her anger. There was fury with herself at the way she had felt about this man adding to the anger in her voice, but she only thought of Fiona. 'Fiona doesn't trust adults,' she continued savagely. 'She has nothing. Her clothes look as if she's been living in some third-rate orphanage. She doesn't even seem to have toys. She hasn't a mother and she hasn't friends and she only has the bits of you that you can spare from your precious work. What sort of a life have you given her, Adam?'

'Christy, I ——'

'I know,' she snapped. She had gone so far now that she found it impossible to stop. The pain in Adam's eyes only built the anger. If he thought he could look at her like that and make her love him. . .make it OK to treat his little girl like that. . .

'I know,' Christy repeated bitterly. 'You couldn't cope with the pain of losing Sarah. You had to get away. You had to leave your responsibilities to find some other life. Only then somehow your responsibilities caught up with you. But I don't think they have, Adam McCormack. You can't be a father to Fiona doing what you're doing. You've been back two days and you've dumped her twice. She's a darling, Adam, and she deserves a father who loves her. If she were my little girl I'd love her to death, even if it meant giving up everything else to do it. I feel that way about her and I've known her for less than twenty-four hours. How can you possibly justify abandoning her when you've had her all her life?'

To her fury Christy found she was crying. She brushed angry tears away from her cheek and turned away. She had no right to say what she had. No right. Fiona had even less rights, she thought bitterly. Someone had to say it. How she had ever thought she could love this man. . .

'You'd give up everything for a child. . .' Adam sounded almost as if he was talking to herself.

'Nothing is more important than people,' Christy said bleakly. 'That's what I was brought up to believe, regardless of what creed you follow. When. . .if I have children, then they would have to come first. My husband and my children before everything else. As Fiona should be before everything in your life. . .'

He moved then. In one swift stride Adam was before her, grasping her shoulders until she cried out in pain. 'You don't mean that, Christy,' he said harshly. 'Do you?'

'Of course I do,' she snapped. 'Let me go.'

'Christy——'

'Excuse me, Miss Blair, but are you open?'

Christy wheeled around, Adam's hands still gripping her shoulders. A woman was standing by the door.

'Kevin's got an ear infection and Dr Blair said he had to have these antibiotics tonight,' the woman said apologetically. She looked pointedly at Adam. 'I can come back if you're busy.'

'That's quite all right, Mrs Hay,' Christy said swiftly. She wrenched herself from Adam's grasp. 'Dr McCormack was just taking his daughter and leaving, weren't you, Dr McCormack?'

He was still staring at her as though he had never seen her before. He looked like a man who had suddenly been handed a gift, and the gift was infinitely precious.

'Did you mean every word you just said, Christy?'

'I've never been more serious in my life,' she said savagely, her anger still pulsating. 'Now leave. I'm busy.'

'I'll leave if you come to dinner with Fiona and me tonight.'

'You have to be joking!'

Adam shook his head. 'Like you, I'm deadly serious. So much so that if you don't agree I'll pick you up now and take you home over my shoulder.'

'With Fiona on your other shoulder?' Christy said sarcastically. 'I'd like to see you try.'

'That's a challenge, if ever I've heard one.' There was sudden laughter in his voice. He turned to Christy's bemused customer. 'Do you think I should try, Mrs Hay?'

'I want my antibiotics,' Mrs Hay laughed. 'Otherwise I'd say go right ahead.' She was clearly intrigued and delighted by the emotional tension in the normally sedate pharmacy.

Adam nodded. 'In deference to Mrs Hay's antibiotics I'll leave you in peace, Christy Blair. But if you are not at my dinner-table by seven tonight. Fiona and I will come looking.' He lowered his voice to a dramatic and threatening growl. 'And this country's not big enough to hide in, Christy Blair.'

CHAPTER THIRTEEN

She didn't go. Of course she didn't go. Christy went home to a cool bath, fed the tired Bounce, made herself a sandwich she couldn't eat and went and sat on the back veranda. The night was hot and still. Down in the town Adam and his daughter would be eating their dinner without her. He surely hadn't been serious when he'd said she was to come.

It seemed he had. At ten minutes past seven Adam's car pulled to a halt outside Christy's cottage. She didn't move. She recognised the sound of the car but from where she was she couldn't be seen. Her front door was locked. Adam could knock all he wanted but she was going nowhere.

It wasn't Adam who came to find her. Bounce had been asleep on her lap. All of a sudden he squirmed, gave an excited woof and leaped to the ground. Coming around the side of the house was Fiona.

She looked different. She was still dressed in those awful clothes, but her hair had been released. It was now bunched in an inexpert ponytail, a mass of curls tied twice with red, koala-patterned hair ribbon. She peered around the house, spotted Christy, gave her ribbons a careful pat as though preparing them for inspection and proceeded. Bounce met her halfway. Fiona greeted him sedately, cast a nervous look behind her to make sure her father was still in sight, and kept going, Bounce bouncing at her side.

'My daddy has made a picnic,' she announced gravely. 'You have to come.'

Christy made herself smile at the grave little girl. 'It's kind of you and your daddy,' she said softly. 'But

177

it's your first proper night in your new home. You and Daddy should enjoy it together.'

Fiona reached out and took Christy's hand, tugging it insistently. 'But we're having a picnic,' she repeated as though Christy hadn't quite grasped the idea. She took a deep breath as though searching for courage. 'Daddy says it's my welcome-home party, and a party's not a party without friends. And he said you might come if I was brave enough to invite you myself.'

'I'll tell you what,' Christy said desperately. 'You can take Bounce.'

Fiona considered this. Finally she shook her head. 'No,' she said. 'Daddy says we need people friends. Bounce is my dog friend. Kimberley is my koala friend. If you don't come I won't have any people friends at all.'

She couldn't do it. Christy stared down at the trusting little girl and she couldn't deny her. A people friend. . . If the price of giving Fiona that was to put up with Adam McCormack for one more night then she'd have to do it. She stood up and looked down at her serviceable skirt and blouse. 'I'm not dressed for a picnic,' she told Fiona helplessly.

'That's OK,' Fiona said serenely. 'Neither am I.'

Adam was standing by the car. He smiled in welcome as his daughter led Christy to him and Christy glared in response. She was being nice to Fiona but her niceness didn't extend to this blackmailing male. She shook her head as he opened the front passenger door.

'No,' she said bitterly. 'I'm sitting in the back.'

'But. . .'

'Fiona's the guest of honour tonight.' Christy ignored Adam and smiled down at Fiona. 'The guest of honour always sits in the front.'

Adam nodded gravely. 'That's true,' he said thoughtfully. He smiled at his daughter. 'I guess as long as we have Miss Blair then it doesn't much matter if she sits on the roof, does it, Fi?'

'She might get blown off,' Fiona said, horrified. Adam appeared to consider.

'Very true,' he said at length. 'Miss Blair, you'll have to content yourself with the rear seat. That or the boot. . .'

He took them to the place on the river where he and Christy had swum before. They drove over the paddocks and came to a halt where the riverbank dropped to the sweeping grey of the river. Fiona was out of the car almost before it had stopped. She hauled open Christy's door and grabbed her hand. For the first time she sounded like a normal, excited child.

'Come and see,' she told Christy. 'We have a red rug and cushions and the lady in the café made us sandwiches and cakes called lamingtons and Daddy brought lemonade and shamp. . .shamp something for you and dog biscuits for Bounce. And Daddy says we can swim.' She frowned. 'Only I can't swim,' she confided. 'But Daddy says he'll hold me.'

It was as she had promised. The picnic had been prepared with care. The food was still tightly locked in the portable coolers but Christy saw that the scene had been set with considerable flair. Each place was set with a bright red napkin. Crystal champagne flutes marked Christy's and Adam's places. There was a bright plastic beaker with fluorescent straw in Fiona's place and for Bounce a red and yellow dog dish with a serviette spread under it. 'In case he dribbles,' Fiona explained solemnly. 'He's really still very young.'

Adam followed them down. He stood listening to his daughter's chatter with a half-smile on his face. In his jeans and open-necked shirt he looked relaxed and happy. Christy caught his look with shock. She had never seen him look like this.

She turned away deliberately, smiled at Fiona and sat down. 'Let's eat, then, shall we?' she said firmly. She cast a glance at her watch. 'I can't stay very long, Fiona. I have work to do at home.'

Fiona's face fell. 'But. . .'

'I wouldn't worry, sweetheart,' Adam told her, opening the coolers. 'Miss Blair is our captive for the night.'

Christy drew in her breath. 'Dr McCormack. . .'

'It's true, Christy,' he told her gravely. 'There's no phone and no taxi for miles. You might as well relax and enjoy our company.'

Despite herself Christy did. She refused to speak to Adam except when absolutely necessary but she soon found that her conversation was hardly required. Fiona spoke for all of them. For once she felt safe and it showed. She chattered happily, filled their plates, scolded them for not eating more and encouraged Bounce to eat one more dog biscuit. After dinner she dug. 'If I'm not careful I'll dig all the way to England,' she announced.

'Don't you want to go back to England?' Christy asked, and a shadow crossed the little girl's face.

'Daddy says we're staying here,' she said firmly and went on digging.

Bounce spent his time joyfully head down and tail up in the hole. Soon, though, his tail drooped downwards. Finally the pup staggered up the bank to Christy's lap and fell asleep.

'You've eaten one too many dog biscuits,' Christy said dubiously, feeling his rotund tummy. 'I don't know about you sleeping on my lap.'

'What on earth are you suggesting?' Adam laughed. 'Bounce knows what laps are for.'

Despite herself, Christy laughed too. The night was insidious with its beauty. The warmth, the gentle sound of running water and the scent of the gums made her anger hard to maintain. Adam smiled at her and it was all she could do not to smile back. . .to lose herself in that smile. . .

'Can we have a swim?' Fiona pleaded. 'Before we go

home. . .' She stopped as a thought stuck her. 'I
haven't a costume,' she frowned.

'Knickers are fine,' Adam told her. 'Aren't they,
Christy?'

'For people under the age of ten knickers are fine,'
she agreed gravely.

Adam pulled off his jeans and shirt to reveal dark
green swimming-shorts. 'I'm more than ten,' he told
his daughter. He turned and dived into the water in
one lithe movement. The water hardly registered his
body entering. He disappeared under the surface and
emerged halfway across the river. 'How about you,
Miss Blair?'

Christy was helping Fiona off with her skirt and
blouse. She looked out to where Adam was standing
on a sandbank, his body gleaming with water, and his
lazy smile mocking. She'd have to be mad. 'I'm not
under ten,' she said firmly. 'And besides, Bounce
considers me his bed.'

She sat and watched as man and child played in the
water. Adam put his daughter on his chest and played
boat to her boatman. For a man who must be dead
tired he seemed to have come alive. Christy watched
and her heart twisted. Her heart had no business to
twist, she thought savagely. She couldn't still be in love
with this man. She couldn't. . .

Finally Fiona came from the water, dripping and
happy. Christy found a towel and rubbed her dry and
then wrapped her in another. The child nestled against
her lap in a gesture of trust and once again Christy's
heart twisted. They sat together as Adam swam long,
slow laps to the curve of the river and back and finally,
like Bounce, Fiona fell asleep.

It was like a drug, Christy thought bitterly. The
warmth, the sleeping little bodies curled into her and
the sight of Adam. . . She wiped away an errant tear
as she touched Fiona's curls. If Adam had been free. . .

If Adam had been free five years before then this little one might be part of her. . .

Then Adam was before her, towelling his muscled body and looking down at Christy and Fiona with love. . . Christy looked up and gasped. There was no mistaking the look on his face and there was no mistaking the fact that the love he was feeling encompassed her.

'Adam, I have to get home,' she said uncertainly, her hands moving to lift the sleeping Bounce so that she could stand.

'No.' He was kneeling before her, his hands grasping hers and holding her down. 'Christy, I have to talk to you. That's why I brought you here.'

'Fiona brought me here,' she said bitterly. 'Otherwise I wouldn't have come.'

'I know.' He smiled ruefully. 'I know that.' He stood again, finished his towelling and pulled on his shirt. Then he sank to sit beside his daughter. From the riverbank they'd seem an ideal couple, Christy thought fleetingly. A man and a woman with a sleeping child between them and a pup. . . She shook the image off angrily. It didn't fit. Not after what Adam had done. . . 'Christy, I want to tell you a story.'

'I don't want to hear.'

'I know,' he said grimly. 'But I need to tell you and I'm not taking you home until you've listened.' He sighed. 'It's unfair, my Christy, but I'm gambling on something important here. You have to listen.'

'I'm not your Christy. . .'

Adam wasn't listening. He was staring out at the slow-moving water and she might not have existed. He was back in England. He was back in a nightmare that had ended his first marriage. . .

'I loved Sarah,' he said into the gathering dusk. The flat words hung over the tiny group on the riverbank. He seemed to have trouble going on from there but eventually the forced words came. 'It was different,

Christy. It was different from how I feel about you but it was love none the less. Sarah had an unhappy family life. Her father had died when she was young and her mother was cold and brutally ambitious. Sarah was doing law but she hated it. We met and married within six months. Sarah's mother was appalled. To marry an impoverished young doctor with no family connections and no ambition past obstetrics was the height of lunacy as far as Helen was concerned. She told Sarah she'd speak to her again after a divorce and not before.'

On Christy's lap Bounce wuffled sleepily. Fiona stirred in response. There was no other sound.

'Sarah didn't seem to mind her mother's coldness,' Adam said bleakly. 'We had each other and that was all that mattered. And then she became ill. . .' His voice tailed off. 'I've already tried to explain the next few years to you, Christy. They were hell. Loving someone and watching them gradually become someone else. . . Well, it was the worst kind of hell I could envisage. I believe I nearly went mad myself. It was only friends like Richard who kept me sane.'

Adam picked up a stone and flung it out into the river. Another followed and another.

'When Sarah was under medication, during one of her more stable periods,' Adam said bitterly, 'she made contact with her mother again and Helen convinced her to file for divorce.' He grimaced. 'That was a bleak time. It was then that Richard picked me up and took me to your home for a week. He said a week of sleep and home cooking would do me wonders. And then you came into my life. . .'

'Adam, I don't want to——'

'Shut up, Christy,' Adam said firmly. 'You're going to hear the whole thing whether you like it or not.' Another stone went the way of its predecessors. 'I can't explain how I felt then,' he said. 'Maybe you know. I think you felt the same current running between us. But for me it was like a window opening to life again.

There were kind, loving families in the world. There were sweet, gentle and sane people. There was you. . .'

'Only then Sarah came,' Christy said bleakly.

Adam threw another stone, this time with force. 'She did,' he said. 'It was as if she was at war with herself, fighting for the Sarah she once had been. She had filed for divorce but suddenly she wanted me. She pleaded for me to give her another chance.' He shrugged. 'She was nearly. . .nearly my old Sarah. I had to try. We spent a week together trying to rebuild something that couldn't be rebuilt. It was a mistake to try. And there was a worse mistake,' he said grimly. 'I believed Sarah when she told me she was on the Pill. She wasn't and Fiona was conceived.'

'Oh, Adam. . .'

'After that week she went again,' Adam said harshly. 'Back to Europe with her mother. The problems became worse. Her mother had her admitted to Europe's most expensive hospitals. I paid the bills but neither Sarah nor her mother would have any other contact with me. When Fiona was born the hospital let me know. I was legally still Sarah's husband and I was paying the bills. When Sarah's mother found I'd been informed of Fiona's birth she moved Sarah and the baby before I could get there.'

'Oh, Adam. . .'

He had ceased throwing stones. He was staring straight ahead and his face was bleak.

'The next few years. . .well, they were a special kind of hell. I had mammoth hospital bills I had to pay. I'm still paying them. And on top of that I had legal bills as I tried to get access to Fiona.' He shook his head. 'If I told you what that woman was capable of. . . Well, sufficient to say that I saw Fiona three times in four years, and each access to her was the result of thousands of dollars in court fees. It went on and on. The divorce came through, and somehow Sarah and Helen were able to persuade the court to give them custody.

Sarah didn't want Fiona. She was past taking care of
her but her mother wanted her. Or rather she wanted
to hurt me. . .'

'So how. . .?'

Adam laughed, a bitter laugh. 'Fate played me lucky
at last,' he said. 'Sarah's mother met and married a
man with a title. She dropped her mad daughter like a
hot cake. I brought Sarah back to London, and she
promptly killed herself.'

'I don't believe. . .'

'Ironic, isn't it?' Adam said harshly. 'I thought I was
doing the right thing. . .'

'And Fiona?' Christy said gently.

'There was another court battle,' he said bitterly.
'Sarah's mother by this time had other things on her
mind than a small granddaughter, but she blamed me
for everything that had gone wrong with Sarah and she
still saw she had the power to hurt me by holding on to
Fiona. She went to court and argued she'd been a
mother to Fiona since she'd been born. She argued I
was occupied with my obstetrics and with the bills I
still had outstanding from Sarah's hospitalisation I
couldn't afford to give up work. She won. The court
gave her custody. I had access but you wouldn't believe
how many valid reasons that woman found for not
giving me access. I could telephone Fiona only.' He
grimaced. 'Do you know how hard it is to maintain any
sort of relationship with a child by telephone?'

'So. . .'

'So I worked myself into the ground for a while,' he
said bleakly. 'And then a letter arrived from Richard
telling me about life in Australia. He mentioned you as
having migrated too. I started thinking about Australia,
and I let myself think of you. . .'

'So you abandoned Fiona to her grandmother,'
Christy said quietly.

'No.' His voice was suddenly forceful. He turned to

Christy, reached out and took her hand. 'I took a hell
of a gamble.'

She stared up at him. His eyes held her, compelling
her to meet his gaze. He was willing her to believe
what he was saying.

'By now I realised that Sarah's mother didn't give a
damn about Fiona. She simply wanted to hurt me. She
had enrolled Fiona at a boarding prep school. . . A
boarding-school! There's only one school taking them
that young, and it was costing a fortune. I simply
refused to pay the bills, and I took myself to Australia.
And waited.'

'Adam. . .'

'The school sent Fiona home when the bills weren't
paid,' he told her. 'And home was with Helen and her
new husband. All of a sudden they had a four-year-old
in the house and they didn't like it one bit. The husband
might be a lord but he wasn't rolling in wealth. He
wasn't going to pay any school fees for a child who had
an existing father. He told his wife that Fiona could
stay with them during the week while they were in
London but he wanted her out of the place at other
times. But I was in Australia. Sarah's mother was
caught with a four-year-old she didn't want.'

'So. . .'

'So she rang me and told me to come and get her.
And I told her I no longer wanted her. . .'

'Adam!'

'I told her I'd met a woman here whom I loved and
wanted to marry. I didn't want to be bothered by a
child. . .'

'You. . .'

'Christy. . .' Adam smiled, and his smile was suddenly boyish and eager. 'Don't you see? As soon as
Helen thought I didn't want Fiona then she decided
the thing she wanted most in the world was to hand her
over to me. She disclaimed responsibility from that
point on. She put Fiona in foster care. She said with

her health she was no longer able to care for her. . .'
He shook his head. 'I admit I had no idea she'd go that
far. The welfare authorities contacted me, and I was
there two days later.'

'Adam. . .'

'So you see. . .'

'Adam, don't go on,' Christy said bleakly. 'I can't
bear it. . .'

'Christy, will you marry me?'

There was absolute silence.

'Why?' she said breathelessly. She closed her eyes.
'No matter what you told Sarah's mother, when you
left for England you didn't want me. Not as a wife,
Adam. . . A lover maybe. But not as a wife. . .'

Adam reached down and picked up his sleeping
daughter. She didn't stir. Gently he laid her behind
him on a pile of cushions. He lifted Bounce from
Christy's lap and laid the puppy beside his daughter.
Then he took Christy's hands in his.

'I was speaking the truth to Sarah's mother,' he said
steadily. 'There was a woman in Australia I wanted to
marry. More than anything in the world I wanted to
marry her. But this lady. . .' He looked down tenderly
at her upturned face. 'My Christy. . . My Christy had
told me she wanted nothing to do with children. She
told me that unequivocally and I was fool enough to
believe her. Until this afternoon when I saw your
anger.' He pulled her into his arms. 'Your anger was
my anger. I saw the fury I've felt and the helplessness
of the past few years reflected in your eyes.' He kissed
her gently. 'I love you, Christy Blair. I've loved you
for five long years and whatever you answer now I'll
keep on loving you. Will you marry me?'

Christy looked up and met his eyes. Within them she
saw all she would ever need to know. There was love,
there was tenderness and there was peace.

She placed her hands around his head and drew him

down to return the kiss. The kiss lasted forever. Forever was now within their grasp.

'Oh, Adam,' she whispered, when words were again possible.

'I'm not asking you to be a full-time mother to Fiona,' he said swiftly. 'I've worked this out in my head. . .'

'Since this afternoon?' she teased.

'Since this afternoon.' He kissed her again lightly on the nose. 'The cottage I'm in now is for sale. It's a magnificent building block. If we were to build the house of our dreams there, two doors from Amy Haddon. . .'

'She'd make a great surrogate grandma. . .'

'Not only to Fiona,' Adam smiled. 'Kate's also lined her up.'

Christy smiled. 'Amy will have two grandchildren. . .'

'And that's only the beginning,' he told her.

She appeared to consider. 'Do you think Kate and Richard will have more children, then?' she smiled, and then at the look in Adam's eyes she laughed. 'Adam, my love,' she said softly, 'the way I'm feeling now Amy could be a grandmother ten times over.'

'Well, maybe that's going to extremes,' he grinned. He held her at arm's length. 'Does this mean you've agreed to marry me, Miss Blair?'

Christy smiled mistily up at him. Her world was a kaleidoscope of joy, spinning crazily around with its epicentre in Adam's eyes.

'Of course I'll marry you, Dr McCormack,' she told him formally. 'Oh, Adam. Oh, my love. . .'

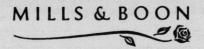

MILLS & BOON

New Look
Love on Call

A few months ago we introduced new look covers on our medical series and we called them 'Love on Call'. We'd like to hear just how much you like them.

Please spare a few minutes to answer the questions below and we will send you a **FREE** Mills & Boon novel as our thank you. Just send the completed questionnaire back to us today - **NO STAMP NEEDED**.

Don't forget to fill in your name and address, so that we know where to send your **FREE** book!

Please tick the appropriate box to indicate your answers. ☑

1. For how long have you been a Mills & Boon Medical Romance/ Love on Call reader?

Since the new covers ☐ 1 to 2 years ☐ 6 to 10 years ☐
Less than 1 year ☐ 3 to 5 years ☐ Over 10 years ☐

2. How frequently do you read Mills & Boon Love on Call books?

Every month ☐ Every 2 to 3 months ☐ Less often ☐

3. From where do you usually obtain your Love on Call books?

Mills & Boon Reader Service ☐
Supermarket ☐
W H Smith/John Menzies/Other Newsagent ☐
Boots/Woolworths/Department Store ☐
Other (please specify:) _____

4. Please let us know how much you like the new covers:

Like very much ☐ Don't like very much ☐
Like quite a lot ☐ Don't like at all ☐

5. What do you like most about the design of the covers?

_____

_____

6. **What do you like least about the design of the covers?**

_____
_____

7. **We now use photographs on our Love on Call covers, please tell us what you think of them:** _____

_____
_____

8. **Do you have any additional comments you'd like to make about our new look Love on Call series?** _____

_____
_____

9. **Do you read any other Mills & Boon series? (Please tick each series you read).**

Mills & Boon Romances	☐	Temptation	☐
Legacy of Love (Masquerade)	☐	Duet	☐
Favourites (Best Sellers)	☐	Don't read any others	☐

10. **Are you a Reader Service subscriber?**

Yes ☐   No ☐

If Yes, what is your subscription number? _____

11. **What is your age group?**

16-24 ☐   25-34 ☐   35-44 ☐   45-54 ☐   55-64 ☐   65+ ☐

THANK YOU FOR YOUR HELP

✉   Please send your completed questionnaire to: ✉

Mills & Boon Reader Service, FREEPOST,
P O Box 236, Croydon, Surrey CR9 9EL

NO STAMP NEEDED

Ms/Mrs/Miss/Mr: _____ CLC

Address: _____

_____

_____ Postcode: _____

mps
MAILING
PREFERENCE
SERVICE

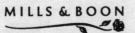

HEARTS OF FIRE

By Miranda Lee

✦ **HEARTS OF FIRE** by Miranda Lee is a totally compelling six-part saga set in Australia's glamorous but cut-throat world of gem dealing.

Discover the passion, scandal, sin and finally the hope that exist between two fabulously rich families. You'll be hooked from the very first page as Gemma Smith fights for the secret of the priceless **Heart of Fire** black opal and fights for love too...

Each novel features a gripping romance in itself. And **SEDUCTION AND SACRIFICE**, the first title in this exciting series, is due for publication in April but you can order your FREE copy, worth £2.50, NOW! To receive your FREE book simply complete the coupon below and return it to:

MILLS & BOON READER SERVICE, FREEPOST, P.O. BOX 236, CROYDON CR9 9EL. TEL: 081-684 2141

NO STAMP NEEDED

Ms/Mrs/Miss/Mr: _____ HOF

Address _____

_____

_____

Postcode _____

mps MAILING PREFERENCE SERVICE